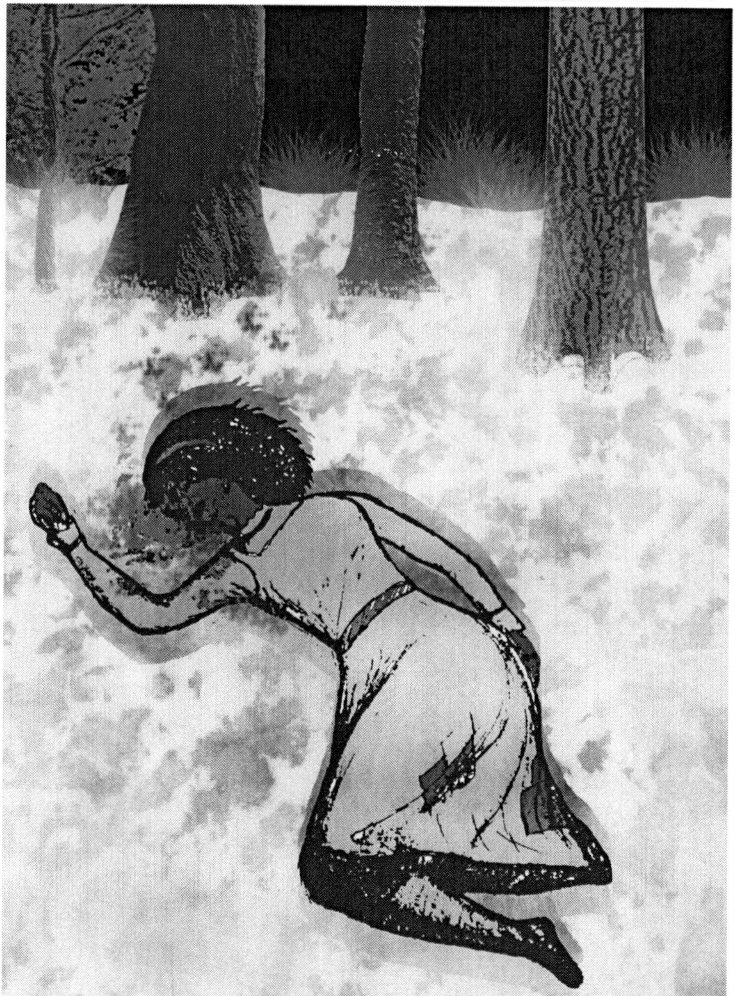

MCTAVISH MANOR

Inés G Labarta

Holland House

Copyright © 2016 by Inés Gregori Labarta

Inés Gregori Labarta asserts her moral right to be identified as the author of this book. All rights reserved. This book or any portion thereof may not be reproduced or used in any manner whatsoever without the express written permission of the publisher except for the use of brief quotations in a book review.

All characters appearing in this work are fictitious. Any resemblance to real persons, living or dead, is purely coincidental. Any characters denoted by government office are entirely fictional and not based on any official, appointed or elected.

Paperback ISBN: 9781910688151
Kindle ISBN : 9781910688229

Cover picture and illustrations: Mireia Ibàñez Cid
Cover design by Ken Dawson, Creative Covers
Typeset by handebooks.co.uk

Published in the UK

Holland House Books
Holland House
47 Greenham Road
Newbury, Berkshire RG14 7HY
United Kingdom

www.hhousebooks.com

Supported using public funding by
ARTS COUNCIL ENGLAND
LOTTERY FUNDED

Para Lucía y Silvia

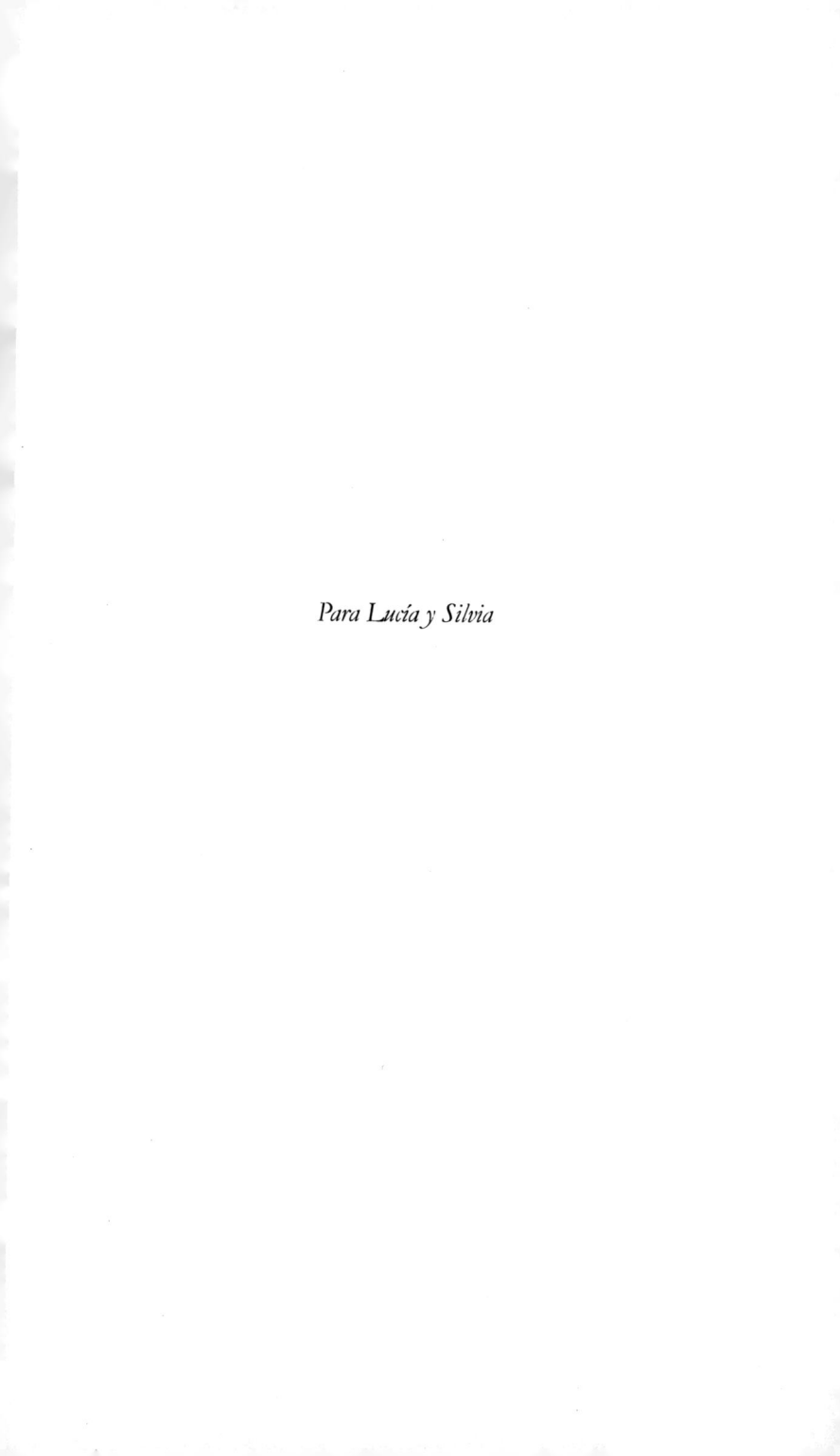

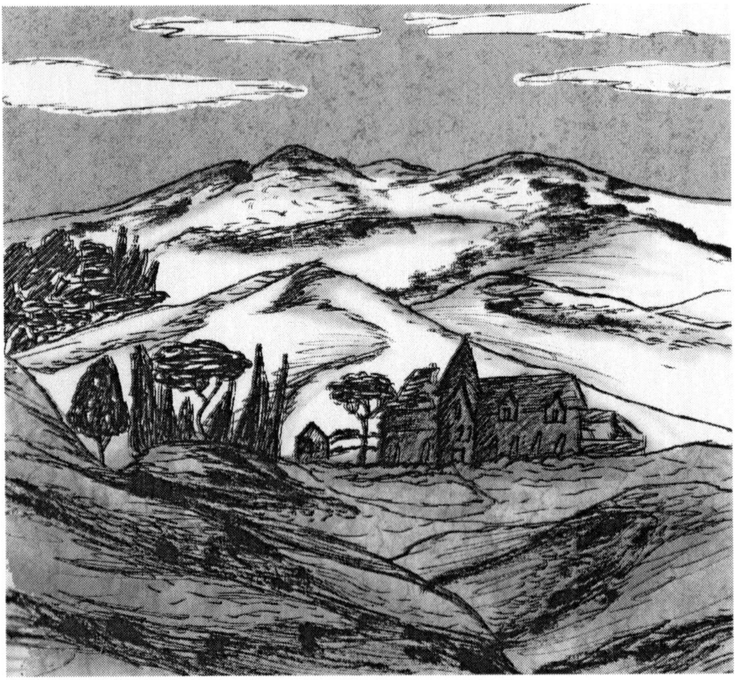

Chapter 1

Glenfinnan,
Tuesday Nov. 29th - Friday Dec. 2nd 1803

My dearest Augusta,

At last I §take my pen in hand to write you these lines, hoping they find you in good health as they leave me at present. Knowing your good heart, you must be so concerned about your wretched cousin, wondering if he survived this dangerous journey up North. Well, I am alive, but deadly ashamed of my carelessness, for after our sorrowful farewell I promised to write every day & now a month is already gone. How can I apologise? Still, no doubt you will be glad to hear that my rural retirement in the Highlands as the McTavish's doctor through the winter is nothing but pleasant & delightful.

The house is majestic. The elements have blackened the stone to give it the romantic and venerable colour of years gone by—certainly as many years as cracks one can count on the walls. The healthy Highlands' wind often swirls inside—but this is not in any way irksome, for it lessens the heaviness of the air that sometimes gives to the house a somewhat oppressive atmosphere. They do not have marble floors as we do, but their wooden ones are very peculiar—when someone steps on them, a primitive melody can be heard—surely a very fine tone, if only I had a musical ear. The parlour, smaller than your little reading room, is full of pictures—I would like to describe them, but I am afraid the smoke of the fireplace has covered the most intriguing parts.

The McTavishes have given me the best room in the whole building—I have to climb up no less than four floors to find this place in which the architect has achieved the seemingly impossible—a chamber right under the roof. It has everything that I need, including a tiny window which delights me with a view of the sublime landscape. In the past I could have considered these endless mountains dull or even bleak, but now they inspire a variety of awe and quietness that eases my so often restless spirit.

The McTavishes are, as you assured me, the kindest people & it is evident at once how much they appreciate our family. They immediately inquired about the future of the Bilsland Bank—do not think they questioned your role as the director—they were merely concerned about your health. They also wondered why I, as the Bilslands' direct heir, have no experience with finance but, beloved cousin, what indeed astounded them most was the fact that both of us remain unmarried!

Their thirteen-year-old twins are sweet angels. The yellow haired one is so generous that he left a dead hedgehog inside my chamber pot the first day I arrived—he assured me it was a present from his pet cat. I have been told by his proud father that he is a capital shot with his Doune pistols—undoubtedly he exercises this skill regularly, for one can smell on his clothes how much pleasure he finds in blood sports. I discovered very recently that 'he' is indeed the wrong pronoun for this twin, as Nature made 'him' of the female kind—although nothing in 'his' appearance or manners would immediately suggest it. I observed this when I saw 'him' swimming in the pools formed in the grounds at the back of the house during a storm—'he' did not seemed bothered at all by the sharp rain or the unbearable resounding of the thunders—perhaps city dwellers like us tend to image girls as fragile flowers to be kept in fine china vases, whereas here in the Highlands the weather shapes the two sexes equally sturdy—heather and bracken, indeed..

The brown-haired twin is the mother's favourite, though. She thinks him perfect & I tend to agree, as the only possible defect in this talented young man is deafness. Because it is somewhat demanding to maintain a proper conversation with him, Mrs McTavish encourages him to interact mostly with one living creature—a white goat she had brought from Duncansburgh recently.

Dinner is usually the most amusing time. We listen to Mr McTavish—not his words, mark you, but the almost canine sounds he emits while ingesting food! Mrs McTavish is talkative & gentle, always making sure I eat enough—I am afraid I may have disconcerted the poor woman when I said I do not consume meat, as she could not offer me anything else but cabbage. I eat this in extremely modest quantities, not because of its brownish colour, but because I do not desire to exhibit a gargantuan appetite. As a doctor, I should set an example for others—food is something that should be taken in moderation. The only exception to this rule might be during pregnancy—Mrs McTavish's current state. She most certainly exhibits an extraordinary appetite, partaking of considerable pieces of meat which look as well preserved as any of the corpses in the Faculty of Medicine in Edinburgh.

Yesterday, Mrs. McTavish asked me why my eyes are black. She has been studying the Scotch race for years, inspired by Hume & Voltaire. When I told her that my mother was French she manifested a keen interest in using me as a subject for the treatise she is writing—& before I could even agree she was already scribbling furiously in her journal. My dear, you did not tell me about the cleverness of our common friend – sharing the same passion for research promises the pleasure of long evenings discussing the nature of humanity & the lower species.

Yet, for all the pleasures of her company, she could never replace you, my dear, my beloved one. Am I bothering you with these words? That is far from my intention.

Do take care of your health. Allow me to set out exactly how you should proceed to contain Consumption. First, have one of the glasses in my studio heated—you will notice they have slightly sharpened edges. Then, when you are alone in your chamber—away from indiscreet eyes—hold tightly the scalpel I left for you & make a small incision in your skin. The cut has to be made under your clavicle, just above the breast. Immediately after, grab the glass—which should still be hot, not warm—& press it on the flesh—your hands must not tremble. I am sure you can perform the treatment—otherwise you would not have allowed your doctor to leave! Remember to take some linen towels with you to protect your garments.

Friday. I will go Duncansburgh to deliver this letter, but before I leave I must tell you of an extraordinary event that challenged my abilities as a physician. On

St Andrew's day we were having a joyful & innocent celebration when the kitten bit the yellow-haired twin & I had to urgently treat the tearful girl. While I was taking care of the haemorrhage, Mrs McTavish trapped the unlucky feline behind the door—& smashed it against the wall!

I shall admit I was impressed & moved by such passionate display of a mother's instinct to protect her offspring—if somewhat taken aback at the ferocity of her actions!

Give my regards to all & please make sure My Father is given something to eat between his drinking.

I am
 Your devoted friend & ever most loving & affectionate cousin,

Charles Bisland MD

P.S. I have met this negress servant you told me about—the one you described as a fascinating witch from a land of Godless myths & superstition. Indeed, our encounter was quite dramatic, as I found her lying in the mud outside the mansion – wolves had attacked her & apparently ate half of her face. You would be delighted to know that thanks to my efforts she has recovered her health—but, sadly, not her left eye.

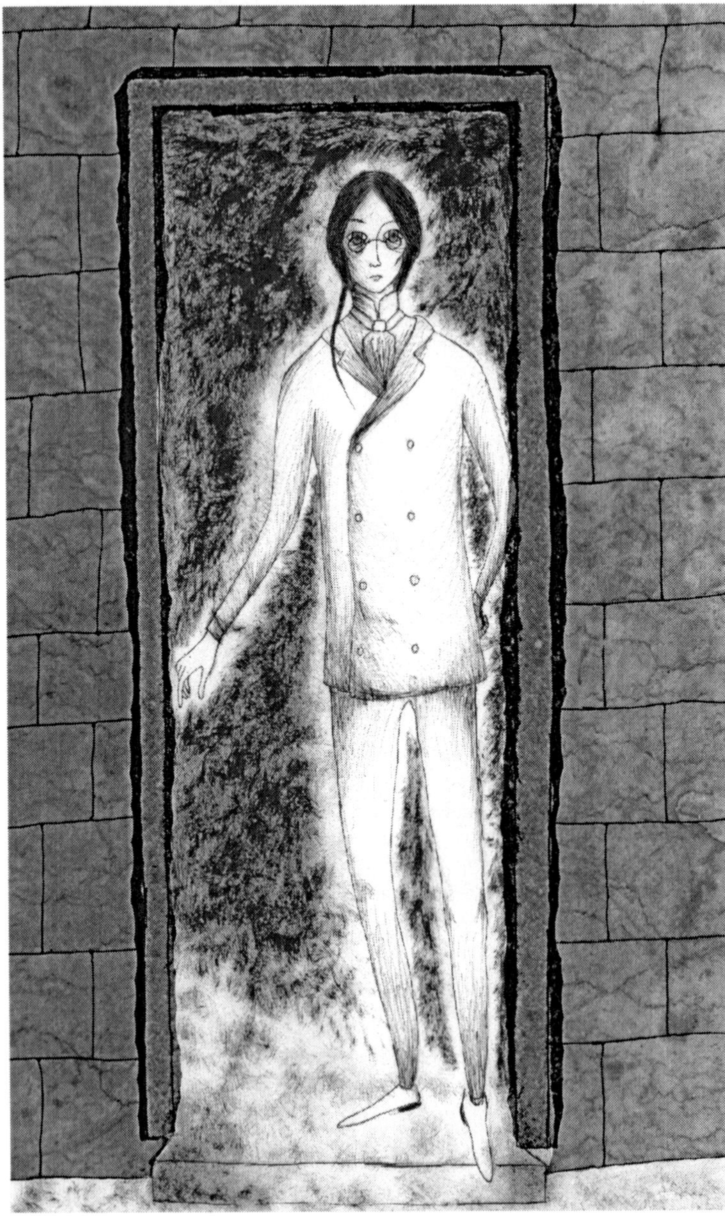

Chapter 2

'Monster let us see it... let us...'

The scullion grabbed my face.

Obatala Oba tasi Obada badá.

'Scar, sca– she stinks like the devil's fart, she stinks like a pig... Look at this, skin like shit... '

The maid hit my arm.

Badanera ye okulaba okual.

'Come here... Take that... Take— Hey, don't try to bite me you monster...'

The scullion pulled my hair with his furry fingers when I was trying to escape.

I cried.

Ache lobo ache ono ache ariku baba Ago.

I called to Obatala, the White God. I knew he would come.

Midnight. In the kitchen, the servants chased me like pine martens. Candles and merriment had banished the usual darkness within, while drunken bawls and flute music joined the wind outside. The air smelt of roasted meat, the floors were sticky with spilled beer and whisky—

You know, I wanted to dress like a lady, so I had mended my gown with straw sacks and decorated it with dried leaves and moss. I'd also made a necklace with pearl mouse bones and snail shells and folded my curls and put auburn walnuts in them. You would tell me I look as beautiful as the goddess Oshun, the One Who Cannot Be Loved Enough, but the others were not impressed. They only wanted to see my *cicatriz*.

The door opened with a bang. We all went silent because this man came from the upper rooms.

'*Òu se trouve la bièrre?*'

The doctor stood on the threshold. He was white: shirt,

breeches, handkerchief and the moon-like skin held by his long, night hair. He wore silver circles around his eyes— did he use them to see beneath the skin to cure people? His hairless cheeks glittered, his pale lips spoke a language nobody could understand. He was not from the ordinary world but from above, where the celestial bodies dance, humming distant songs.

Obatala, the White God.

'No beer, then...'

The doctor kicked the floor and the wood complained. He laughed. We all remained still. I was the only one who dared to look at him. Eye to eye. When he moved towards me, the scullion and the maid stepped back.

The doctor took off my bandage. He cleaned and placed it there hours ago in the clarity of the morning.

The lavender pink of the raw flesh.

The snake-path of black stitches crimson-edged, brown where blood had turned into a dry scab. [The maid covers her mouth with both hands but the doctor looks amazed, as if he is observing the metamorphosis of an exotic larva.]

'Puis-je avoir le plaisir de cette danse ma sublime dame?'

He bowed and opened his arms. I went inside. Although his skin was cold and wet, his embrace was warm and smelt alcohol-sweet. He swung round, he sang and danced with me, he sped up, one quick turn, another [—we are about to crash into the baking oven—we swirl around the large table in the middle of the kitchen—we hit a pile of copper pots—a rattle—]

He laughed and sang louder and louder until his cheeks were rotten raspberries and I couldn't breathe but I was happy and laughed too because I felt like I was flying and the pain was gone.

The doctor stopped abruptly.

'Adieu, my boring fellows.'

He kept a grip on my arm as we went out of the room.

We ran through the house's forgotten veins, and took the stairs down to the cellar. It smelt of dried roots and putrid weeds.

'Why here, Doctor?' [I said 'Doktór', I hear it now]

He had been taking care of me for two months, but this was the first time I spoke to him.

'The boat.'

'Boat?'

'It's about to depart.'

The cellar was so dark that I was afraid of losing my own body [it vanishes in the shadows and I cannot find it—].

'Don't like boats, doctor.'

My heart was loud.

'Don't like them. '

'Have you taken one before?' he asked me.

'Don't like them.'

I wanted to leave but he pushed me down. In the darkness he was not white anymore, but a dangerous shadow in which I might—

'Shh...'

The doctor sat down, wrapping his arms around me. It calmed my shivers.

'People in boats, evil.' I pressed my wet eye against his handkerchief. '

I took one, long, long ago. It was big and crowded, the sea and the mist were one... one shadow. My mother said... *Froid*, she said that was the first time we felt it.' He rocked me.

'Don't like boats, people...' The distant sound of the rain drowned my words. 'They took me...' I wanted to tell him everything. About how we embarked on Puerto de Vigo believing we'd reach another world called the Americas. 'People staring... I can't move. *Hermano*... brother was there too. They took me, but I invoked Oshun, and the storm came, and then the boat... *bum*... The boat went down and we were dying because they were evil and I cursed them.' The rain's sound blended with my breathing. 'The three men that took me, I remember all his faces, I'll—'

'We're safe.'

The doctor caressed my face and fondled my damaged skin, his fingers like a breeze. Then he spoke and I heard him and felt his words in his chest

'This boat is taking us to warmer lands, away from the Winter, see? It will go around the entire world, through light and noise but for us it'd always be this blessed nothingness.'

Silence.

'You know, I'm thinking about something,' the doctor whispered in the cellar. 'I'm thinking I like it here. I'm not going out when we arrive. The world is beautiful and savage, sure, but I prefer this, safe and warm and wet. The boat can see the exotic lands, and I'll be here imagining them.'

His deep voice reminded me of the ocean's song we used to feel when we lived in *Isla*. My limbs softened, and my eye closed, I was exhausted. We cuddled each other for [— this minute? —this hour?]

I felt two little paws scratching my gown. The Yellow Twin's kitten. The animal appeared petrified. Something was wrong with it. I took the doctor's arms off me and tried to leave, but the creature dragged after me, sobbing like a baby who has been abandoned in the snow.

Abiku.

A hollow spirit looking for an empty receptacle to possess it. And devour it. Padre told us about it.

I rushed up the stairs, past the kitchen, climbed another

flight of stairs and crossed the forbidden threshold into the main corridor. I hid behind a moth-eaten velvet curtain.

The Yellow Twin appeared, the racket from the parlour trailing behind her. Her hair glistened with meat sauce and she had lost one of her shoes. Crouching on the floor, she approached her pet cat.

'Come here...'

The girl dragged it into her arms. Its eyes were two golden orbs that seemed to contemplate invisible stars.

'What? What? Cannot hear you...'

She shook it, and without warning, the *abiku* started controlling the kitten [it wails like a barn owl] and it bit her. The Yellow Twin's screams brought the Mother. She ran to the girl and held her arm.

'Quick' the Mother yelled at the doctor, who was coming from the stairs.

The girl started shaking.

'Here, my child, let me see...'

The doctor bent over Yellow Twin.

The Mother chased the kitten until it hid behind the door, cawing raven-like. It had been haunted by the *abiku* and the Mother knew it too because she banged the door trying to smash the kitten.

'Stop it, for God's sake!' the doctor shouted at the Mother.

He ran to hold the door, but the edge knocked his face. The Mother stepped back with a smile on her face. The kitten disappeared down the corridor [fly, fly kitten]. There were blood-drops on the Mother's dress. [My heart is bursting when I realise that the *abiku* climbed up her legs and entered her womb where her baby dreams].

Abiku, I called it in my mind, *abiku, are you there?*

The doctor swayed. There was a cut above his eyebrow and blood was flooding his face. The silver circles had fallen. He stuck out his tongue for a second, tasting the first red bead that touched his lips then trembled, and it seemed he would fall, would faint. Was he afraid of his own blood? Red and white, his hair like night— Drops were falling and exploding on the floor like new-born stars. I counted them silently.

Uno, dos, tres, cuatro... Sixteen.

Sixteen. Obatala's magic number.

6ft 3in?
33 - Paris, 9th June 1770
- Black Haired European Var:
black oily hair & iris with
corresponding hue.
- Complexion: marble
white
Temperament:
Choleric & Melancholic. Argues passionately. Prefers solitude.

Chapter 3

29th October

At last, the doctor is here. He found my *dubh* wounded in the mud. I had already bathed & cleaned the blood off Cinnamon. My poor child. The weather has turned very bad. I have realised that cold & especially the presence of rain bring my son's disorientation. I will keep him at home, close to the fireplace. He enjoys watching the flames.

Lately, Cinnamon has shown an interest in my *dubh*. I am concerned about this. His body has already adult features. It is natural for him to feel a strong instinct for reproduction. I should find the solution for this soon.

Later. I kept it inside a jar. It is an interesting piece the one Cinnamon took.

31st October

My *dubh* will survive. I am glad. She is unique. I need her. I will keep Cinnamon away from her.

The doctor must be skilled. Miss Bilsland told me he saved her from dying of Consumption 2 years ago. Her father died from the same disease. The Bilslands' nerves are too highly strung. I am certain this is due to their extravagant lifestyle in Edinburgh.

The doctor has spent 3 days looking after my *dubh* in his own room. I told him there is plenty of space in the servants' quarters. He insisted on keeping her in a ventilated apartment.

The doctor's treatment:

> A basketful of withered poppies.
> Cut their heads & pierce their capsules with a sewing needle.
> Add
> 6 chamomile dried flowers.
> 7 grains of ginger.
> 15 grains of rhubarb root.
> Boil it slowly until all the water is gone.
> Add sugar & wine to make the mixture liquid.

He made my *dubh* drink this before he sewed her face. He placed her head on his lap & reconnected the layers of skin. He only stopped when she moaned too loudly. Then he held her hand tightly & whispered meaningless words to calm her. She had her right eye open all the time—she has lost the left one.

Turmeric killed 20 squirrels today. I am very proud of my small warrior. She wanted to give one to my *dubh*. For her to heal, Turmeric said. I had to explain my daughter that Negroes do not eat meat.

7th November

My *dubh*'s fever is dropping. The doctor feeds her with his special wine, warm water & potato soup. It is good Cinnamon cannot see her. He will forget her soon. I am still trying to find a solution for his instincts.

10th November

I have found 2 novels hidden under the doctor's bed. *The Adventures of Ferdinand Count Fathom* & *Memoirs of a Woman of Pleasure*.

13th November

My *dubh*'s skin is healing quickly. I want to take some samples. I am convinced that Negroes exceed all other races in the firmness & density of their fabric – they were created to survive the extreme heat of the dark continent.

Later. The doctor did not allow me to approach my *dubh* when I told him about my idea. I think he did not understand the purpose of my experiment. I must explain it more carefully. For the moment, I have advised him to read *Systema Naturae* by Linnaeus.

Mo duine likes the taste of my breasts when I am pregnant. I like his tang after hunting. Sweat, blood, mud.

14th November

I took some samples from my *dubh*'s skin. The doctor was in the stables taking care of his horse. It is surprising how much time he dedicates to this beast. The first day, I questioned why someone would bring such an expensive animal to this place. By the end of winter, we might need to sacrifice it for food.

Observations about my dubh's *skin sample.*

The chorion is thick with tiny interstices filled with fat.

The cutaneous reticle has a layer of mucous

substance.

The colour depends on the fluid contained in the capillary tubes.

16th November

I found the solution for Cinnamon.

21st November

The doctor has very thin wrists with blue veins prominent. I advised him to eat meat, as it provides strength & helps relax the nerves. If he did so, he would not need to wear spectacles. Yet he had the effrontery to suggest that the excessive intake of animal flesh can also lead to illness! The doctor might have impressed *mo duine* with his flowery language & sparkling instruments, but if he refuses the obvious he might end up developing Consumption like Miss Bilsland. That would be a pity as he would have to leave my house.

25th November

My *dubh* can eat so I have sent her back to the servants' quarters. She needs routine. It took me 16 months to tame her.

I cleaned Cinnamon's tympanic cavity. He complained somewhat. Although he is a strong boy, like his father, he is not very fond of the teasing needles. Tonight, I drew a story for him & Turmeric. We sat beside the fireplace, their heads on my lap, so I could smell their hair. They love when I draw merlins flying.

1st December

The kitten bit Turmeric yesterday, but the doctor prevented me from killing it. He is showing a unmanly weakness for animals—his horse, my *dubh*, the kitten. I told *mo duine* to shoot the kitten if he sees it wandering around. I have to get something for my dear Turmeric. She is very sad since she cannot play with her kitten anymore.

Later. I let Turmeric play with some craniums from my collection.

5th December

I asked the doctor why he wears only white—quite a peculiar colour for a physician. He replied that it forces him to be precise to not stain his clothes.

9th November

The doctor thinks he is here to help me deliver the baby. As if I was not able to cope with the process of giving birth. He has been following me through the house all week trying to examine me with his vaginal speculum. In the end, I allowed him to use it, but only to satisfy my curiosity.

    He is such an interesting specimen to study. Scotch & Norman blood flow through his veins. Along with my *dubh*, he is to be the subject of my research on the reproduction of blood contaminated species.

13th December

It is working. Cinnamon goes to the barn frequently, which is good for his mood.

15th December

I have observed that the doctor has irregular sleep patterns. Noises come from his room—a girl weeping? The wind through the open window? Tonight a disturbing wail woke me up. When I went there, I found him sitting on the bed, wearing his evening clothes, extremely relaxed. He assured me he had not heard a thing. He was smoking poppies.

22nd December

Observations about the doctor:

33 – Paris, 9th June 1770

> 6ft 3in?
> Black Haired European Variety – black oily hair & iris with corresponding hue, analogous to a light coated horse with black tail & black mane.
> Complexion – marble white.
> Temperament – choleric & melancholic.
> Argues passionately.
> Prefers solitude.
> Doesn't indulge in hunting – or other manly sports – prefers to read inside.

28th December

My *dubh* has some strategies to discourage sexual attention from the scullion – she is young, no more than 14 or 15, so naturally her body is a trigger for mating. She goes to the stable very early in the morning to collect horse excrements & spread them all over her skin. Then, men do not approach her. I brought her to my studio & showed this to the doctor. I explained to him these procedures are similar to other strategies that have been largely observed in animals like venomous caterpillars.

Later. The doctor is making a great fuss because the scullion bit the maid in the kitchen. I know the scullion hits my *dubh*. It bothers me if he hurts her badly because I don't want her damaged. But this is the first time the scullion has behaved violently against the other women. These ignorant servants always get nervous when the winter comes, for they cannot go to church or the taverns in town. I need to take care of the situation. The maid has lost most of her right ear.

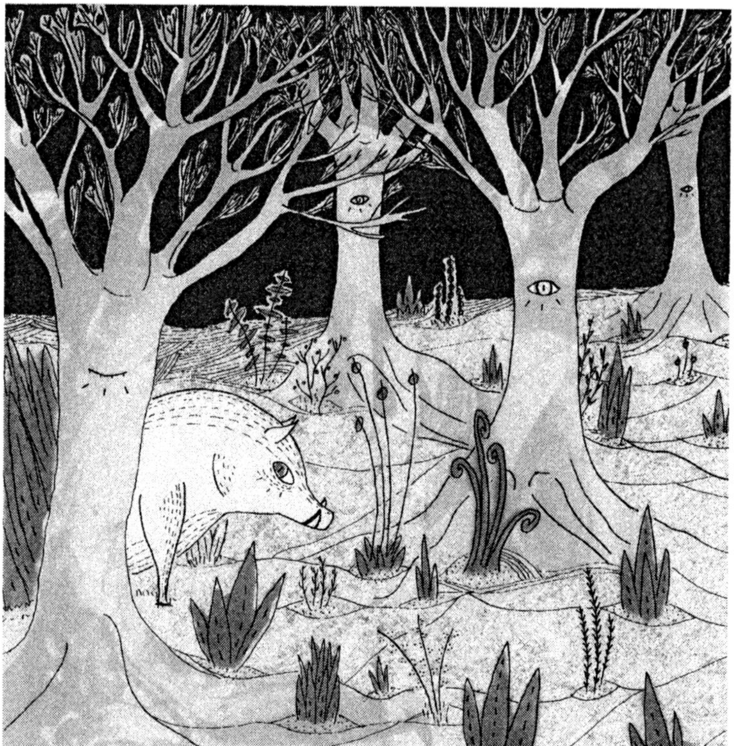

Chapter 4

'There is a wild boar in these woods,
Dellum down, dellum down,
There is a wild boar in these woods,
He'll eat your meat and suck your blood.'

The Yellow Twin and I sang to cover the noises that had been following us all the way from the woods to the house. Cold froze my heart. I looked behind me. Sharp stones. Streams of water that ran away. There were footsteps in the mud, marks of something that was wandering around. [Are we not alone?]

'Bangrum drew his wooden knife
Dellum down, dellum down,
Bangrum drew his wooden knife,
And swore he'd take the wild boar's life.'

The sky was darker. In Winter, dusk came as silent as Iku, The Death. The colossal clouds threatened to fall. The trees were dancing skeletons. A distant wail. The wind? It had to be the hostile wind. [The Mother is hostile like a wild boar, *Hermano*, face framed by reddish yellow hair, cunning eyes the colour of the Highlands' mist]

'The wild boar came in such a flash,
Dellum down, dellum down,
The wild boar came in such a flash,
He broke his way through oak and ash.'

The Yellow Twin was the only member of the family I liked.

Sometimes she put spiders in my gruel, but mostly she was curious and just wanted to play. She helped me carry water from the river, because the Mother wouldn't drink from anywhere else. The servants said the woods were full of monsters like the wild boar of our song. But I was more afraid of those who waited for me inside the house.

Again, again, again I looked behind. The discomfort in the deep of my stomach was not painful like hunger, but like poison. My *cicatriz* itched more than usual. I wanted to get rid of the bandage and scratch it.

'Wolves ate you...'

The Yellow Twin giggled, showing two missing teeth. She reminded me of a small rat with a golden coat and a pink tail.

I was sure wolves didn't eat my eye. Animals are wise, I respect them. They are not like this thing that had been chasing us since we left the river. If only I could find my lost eye. That was where all my memories were trapped.

'Come, come.'

I held the Yellow Twin's hand and ran. If the Mother had seen me touching her she would have punished me. But the mountains were blind, and the trees mute. I could have abandoned her there. I could have offered her to the beast that was following us and nobody would have known.

'I don't—'

She threw her bucket of water but I didn't stop. We were now in the edges of the dead wood. [Something is wailing.] We rushed, and the trees moved along with us. [No birds in the sky, the wind is quiet.] The house was an untouchable shadow.

Again I looked back and I saw him.

Thin and greenish-grey like the trees, he staggered, head down. He wore a frayed shirt and his legs were turning purple from the devouring cold. The scullion's mouth was watery and his eyes white as the mountains. The Yellow

Twin took his fire bird out and made it roar. The air was poisoned with sour black powder and the scullion gasped but didn't move. Instead, he scratched his right arm until black blood ran down. He wept. I wept too that day the Mother separated us in Leith's Port. The Yellow Twin screamed and I threw my bucket against the scullion. He stepped back when he felt the water. We ran away.

[The scullion's wails gnaw at my heels.]

The doctor pressed a tea towel against what was left of the maid's right ear.

'He's ill, cannot you see he's not himse—'

'He frightened my child and attacked the maid.'

The Mother was a raging boar enclosed in the kitchen. Her tartan dress was the only colourful thing on her, as even her face was shaded with a frown of indignation. The cook clutched a bloodstained trivet while the Housekeeper held a steamy drip pan as if it was a shield. The Yellow Twin, cheeks painted with red spots, hit the scullion with a pestle. He lay on the floor but didn't shake or scream anymore. His mouth, chin and neck were white, as if he had been eating cold *nieve*.

'Hold this,' the doctor said to the maid, whose face was turning grey. He went to grab the Yellow Twin.

'Stop.'

'No!' the Yellow Twin screamed. 'He's bad, bad, bad—'

The Yellow Twin struggled to get free of the doctor's grip. When the Mother approached them he let her go. She placed an arm over her daughter's shoulders.

The doctor stared at us. 'He's ill, I have to take care of him—and look in what state he's now, I won't allow—'

'He's to leave the house. Now,' said the Mother.

Outside, the rain started pouring, beating against the walls and windows.

'I'll take him upstairs. He's already lost too much—'

'No, he is to leave the house now.'

'He'll stay with me. I won't leave him like this, I won't admit anymore of this… Some help here, please. Help.'

None of us moved. The doctor tried several times to lift the body. His white waistcoat was getting dirty. In his eyes, always looking at the Mother, I recognised a very familiar emotion: hatred.

'You, come here.'

The doctor called me and I wished I could melt, like the *nieve* that had turned into dirty water on the kitchen's floor.

'Help me, come on, move.'

'She cannot carry much more than one bucket of water.'

The Mother laughed, and jolted me in The doctor's direction. The Yellow Twin hummed the wild boar's song.

The doctor took the shoulders and I held the legs. There wasn't much of the scullion left in that silent body. He always tried to slip his hands under my dress and when I fought back he hit me until I screamed loud. Then he smiled and walked away, as if the act had been somehow consummated. I wanted him dead. And now I was holding him, vulnerable like a baby.

[We climb the narrow staircases and walk through the dark corridors. Dusty velvet curtains cover the walls like shrouds.]

'Here… careful… almost there… careful…'

When we reached the doctor's chamber he placed the body on his own bed. He used his handkerchief to clean the scullion's torn face.

'Basin.'

The doctor didn't look at me.

I moved through the room. There were some glittering instruments in a black case. [I am a child looking at the stars for the very first time.] The basin was placed on a three legged table in the corner. The candles reflected the light in the mirror next to it. Through the glass I saw the doctor bending over the scullion, holding his wrist.

'He's dead.'

There was sour surprise in his voice.

I filled the basin with cold water from the pitcher. He turned when he heard my steps.

'He—'

The doctor dropped the scullion's wrist and snatched the handkerchief.

I waited.

'Go down and get the maid.'

The maid would be too afraid of staying in the same room as the scullion, even if he was dead, but I said nothing. Without dropping the handkerchief, the doctor looked through the window. The blackness stared back at him.

I put the basin in the corner of the bed. I didn't want to leave the room, the only place in the house where I felt safe, so when I came out I stayed by the closed door, feeling the wood on my fingertips. Will the White God try some magic now? Will he discover that I'm responsible for the scullion's death?

[Last moon I saw the *abiku* hiding inside the Mother's belly. Now he sleeps beside her baby but sometimes, *Hermano*, during my dreams, I wake it up and beg it to take everyone in the house. I promise it warm bodies full of yellow fat and fresh blood. I describe for it the delicate form of the bones under the skin, the delicious agony in the screams of those who suffer. Don't you want to play with their bodies, listening to the melodies they produce as if they were bells? You can chew everything you want, my dear *abiku*, eat everything until nothing is left so I can find my eye. Just leave my eye.]

A breaking noise. Trembling, I knelt down to look through the keyhole.

The doctor was wandering around the room like a trapped seagull in a cave. He kicked the chair and it knocked against the table. One of the glittering instruments fell off. Water flowed on the floor, and the sixteen pieces of the china basin were like tiny grey boats sailing on it. The flames of the candles shivered with a sudden breeze. The doctor stopped, taking the bloody handkerchief to his mouth and sucking it thirstily. I couldn't see his face because his hair swung over it, like a dark veil. I just heard him. Sucking.

Then, I knew it.

Obatala quiere sangre.

The White God wants blood.

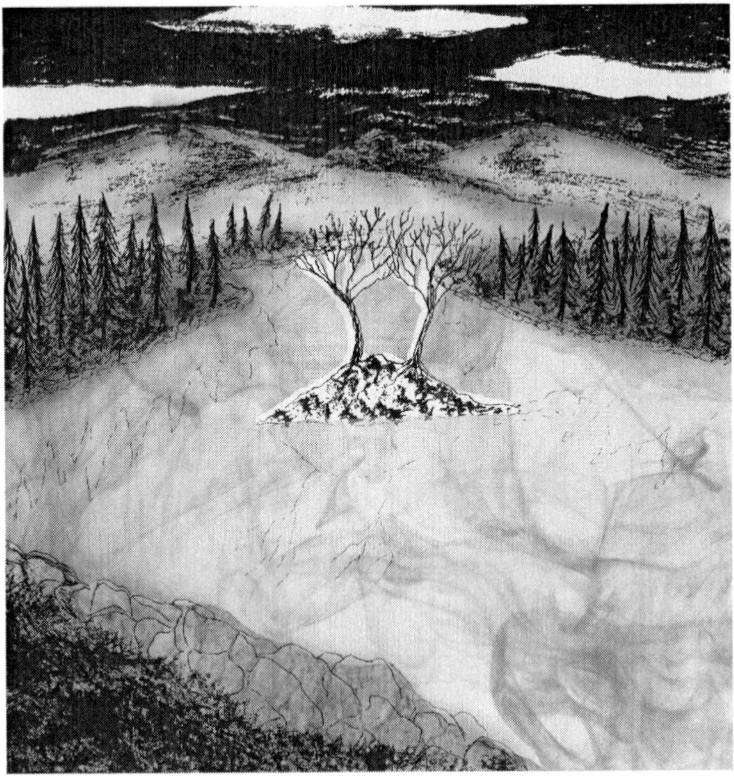

Chapter 5

~~Syrup~~
~~violets 1oz~~
~~jujebes 1oz~~
~~poppies 1oz~~
~~Poppy water 8oz~~
~~Aqua mirabilis 1dr~~
~~Small cinnamon water 1dr~~

Glennfinnan, Saturday ~~31~~ Tues. 2nd Jan.

~~Dearest,~~
Dearest Augusta,
 This thought fills my heart with horror, although it is only before you, my true friend, that I will admit it. Here I am, the only rational soul, if I let myself go with sentimentalism then I will not see the arrival of spring, because oh dear, The Highlands are not made for those with a weak spirit—I am sure that Harley, Mackenzie's dearest son, would not have survived here a day—but you already knew that when you sent me here, am I wrong? I would have put an end to my life that our night, but that solution seemed too ~~simple, too sweet~~ cowardly for all the sins that I have committed. I deserve this purgatory punishment in this mansion under the mountains.
 I am sorry, dear, that my last letter disturbed you. ~~So sorry~~. Sincerely sorry. Yes, I was angry at you when I wrote it. You wounded me that night in your reading room. I remember how you said it, every word of it, our

31

friend Mrs McTavish requires your help in the case of her pregnancy & I firmly believe you should go to her promptly & without delay. Was it necessary, however, to throw the china vase at me? Promptly & without delay. There was water, ~~blessing water~~ flowing onto the floor, reaching the tip of my shoes. I did not dare raise my eyes. ~~Water, oh, how I would like now to d~~ Was it necessary to defend yourself as if I was an animal unable to contain my impulses?

I am perfectly aware of the obligation of keeping a respectable status in both our house & the bank. Your loyal employee Mr Gillespie & my Father & his new wife—this Rose Gibbon you hate so much ~~I agree she is like a jumpy bull~~. I will always be grateful to you, my loving & concerned cousin, you were a mother to me when I was only a little, miserable child, everyday looking after me, making sure I took my crimson medicine. 11. 11 are the years between us as you remind me **ad nauseam**. Yet for me this means nothing. I am a man in all rights & you the woman I love & do not regret what I said that night because I still want to marry you.

18. 18 most probably. Barely 18. He was not the kindest person in the world, God knows that. He used to mistreat the female servants, especially the youngest one. I have complained to Mrs McTavish so many times, yet this wicked woman tortures the wretched girl too. I want to grab Mrs McTavish's shoulders & strike her face until her white skin turns violet, but then I remember I am the monster because what I do is thousand times worse than her sad scientific experiments.

Yes, you also maintain than Negroes are not at all

different to the great apes, but I have travelled all over this continent & the new one & opened enough human beings to know that viscera are always the same no matter the skin colour or the features. The organs are transparent grey & the muscles brown & ~~the blood~~ I saw his blood before he died, screaming under the blows from the other servants. It was too late when I came. His eyes were white & twisted & his mouth was foaming. I am quite certain, tolerably certain, he was poisoned & that intoxication sharpened his violent instincts. But of course, here in the house Mrs McTavish does not believe in my medicine, only in her old-fashioned science books, the same ones my father used to bring her when she was a child—probably this particular choice was a product of alcohol, as so many things in the life of the great Mr Bilsland. I wonder—don't you?—what would he think about this orphan girl turned scientist whose university has been lonely hours in everlasting winters in these wild mountains.

I cleaned him & dressed him in my clothes, trying to hide the colour of death, the smell & marks of my postmortem research. I had spent the night before removing the liver & the pancreas—which did not present any anomaly—& examining carefully everything in his stomach. I only took out two handfuls of white cabbage soaked in a liquid that my nose identified as ale. I cleaned the tissue & the yellow mucus, finding that the viscous bile was muddy green & blueberry violet, as I expected. Nothing strange, nothing surprising, not a single hint. No answer.

I buried him. Nobody wanted to help me. I carried the

body from the dark golden mountains riding Seagull—my poor friend spends all his days in the stable. I wanted the wretched boy to rest away from the bony trees & the wind that sharps the valley. I wanted somewhere beautiful. The Lake. The dark fir trees seemed the spines of a creature for some ancient myth. The horizon showed a pale yellow light, shallow promises of escape. In the water I saw another world dancing through magical currents.

I carried the body to the shore, where the ground was soft & the water cold. I could smell the salty essence of the sea & hear the ravens cawing. I dug a grave with my bare hands. I saw the dead boy lying there ~~*& I desired so much*~~ *There was no snow, just coldness. Streams descended from the top of the Mountains, which have been observing the world since it was born & I hankered to cover their eyes so they would not be able to look at me… I moaned because I tasted him when doing his autopsy & I could not stop myself… Why has nature let this boy die whilst it keeps me alive?*

In the middle of the Lake there ~~*was this*~~ *is a grey little island & over it 2 nude trees, curving & writhing due to the cruel impulse of life, 2 black monstrosities united in forced marriage as nothing else could grow on the scarce space of the rock. Condemned to stay forever together, condemned to share their grief trapped in the nothingness of the black water surrounding them.*

A corpse into the water, putrefaction, I know, but I needed to wash away this sin ~~*the way I licked*~~

I covered him, his young face & ~~*I think I cried, but not*~~

~~for sen~~

I am not sentimental, you know that, it was the intense pain in my chest, I tried to breathe but I could not & my lungs claimed air & they were like 2 ivy branches smashing my ribs & ~~I could not avoid the te~~

I covered his face, but I still see it in my dreams, & even the poppies are useless, I feel the horror darkening my sensations, like the girl from the Under City, oh God, will He forgive us for what we have done? I love you, & I should do so forever, my sins will be my burden for eternity but my love for you will not fade, no matter the distance, no matter the time you live away from me.

10. We were 10 in the house & now we are just 9.
  The scullion boy is gone. He's dissolving in the Lake.
~~This thought fills my heart with h~~

Forever yours,

Charles Bilsland, MD

Chapter 6

The cook handed me a plate of pink meat and sent me to the doctor's room.

You like being his whore, don't you?

The maid would have mocked me if she had seen this. She was an undernourished weasel confined to bed now. The cook said that since the scullion's attack she could not move any part of her body, not even her tongue. [I know it is the *abiku*, feeding on her, sucking her skin when everyone else is asleep. The maid's body gets smaller while the Mother's belly gets bigger.]

'Must tell us what's going on with the doctor, if he's—'

'If he's ill don't come back to us, we don't want to catch it too. Understood?' said the Housekeeper.

This piece of meat was fatty and smelt of onions, wine and spices. It was too big to be from a squirrel. Perhaps a wild dog? Cat? I had seen the Cook working early in the morning; red hands holding a butcher knife, floor covered by small bones and grey fur.

I climbed the servants' staircase. I was used to the broken shape of the steps, like an old man's set of teeth. Water drops fell all the time. I breathed the badness in the walls, the mould, the death. On the second floor, a small cry penetrated the darkness, and a stronger voice echoed down the stairwell. The Mother. The hairs on my arms rose. My foot hit something, the door to the low corridor at the top of the house. Ignoring the warning of the creaking hinges I walked in.

The pale, ill sun entering through the skylight shone in the Brown Twin's hair and hurt my eyes. He always stayed in the forbidden rooms. He was facing away from me—I didn't remember his features—I scratched my *cicatriz*—sweat in my armpits and on my upper lip—the plate about to slip from my hands—he couldn't hear me—I pressed my shoulder against the wet wall [if only I could merge into the stone]. One step on the faded red carpet—another—I needed to reach the door beside him.

I'd only be safe in the doctor's room.

The Brown Twin sat on the floor with his legs crossed. His hands were big but still childish. His ears were covered with bandages. He was playing with a strange thing, like a weapon, a totem, that had a slim part of brass colour and a square wooden base. The boy smashed it on the floor several times. Splinters flew everywhere. Then he hit it against his ears and red spots appeared in the bandages. He was trying to break the metal part, and threw the barrel against the wall several times. When a piece of crystal exploded, I recognised the mutilated object. It was what the Mother used to put her eye in to see things that no one should see.

The rattle strengthened the violence he inflected upon the brass creature. If these hands grabbed me, *Hermano*, I would experience a similar fate. The Brown Twin smelt of goat's dung when I passed by him.

I forget knocking on the doctor's door before entering.

The window was covered with a blanket, so my eye had to get used to the dull light. The mattress was thrown on the floor, and the the bed was like a wooden skeleton. The sheets, dirty with coal dust, were bunched inside the fireplace. The chair was upside down, like a dead horse. The table was bare, and the glittering tools were spread all over the floor, as if running from something. Pieces of paper with writing on were hanging everywhere, like insect wings. On the three legged table, the mirror showed single candle sticks and the pitcher without its parter the basin. The room smelt of ash, piss and rotting lemons.

The doctor was under the table, holding his knees like a child. His eyes were dark holes in his grey face, his hands were bruised and stained with dried mud.

[He is naked.]

'You not good? She said to bring this for you, doctor.'

I held out the meat.

'Oh God... put that aw—'

His body bent. He grabbed the chamber pot and spewed. While he was recovering his breath, I stared at the yellow bile on his chin.

'Don't look... Go away,'

I didn't move.

'Go away, go away, go aw—'

He started vomiting again.

When the doctor's illness was finally discovered by the Mother, I was not allowed to enter the kitchen.

'Don't touch our food, don't touch us, *dubh*. Go to the doctor and take care of him. Just tell me in case he doesn't breathe anymore.' The Mother spoke in a funny voice because she was holding a scented handkerchief against her mouth.

I knew who had done this. The *abiku* craved anything shining and, like a moth, he fluttered to Obatala's brightness. As with the maid, the creature had been sucking the White God every night. Perhaps it started with a few drops but *abikus* cannot be wise or cautious. [You know how they are, hollow spirits who will swallow anything to fill their bottomless need.] It must have survived by gulping down rivers of light from Obatala's moonwarmth, and when it got even more thirsty it surely crept into Obatala's stomach through his navel and settled there. And now the White God couldn't throw it up, because the *abiku* was holding to his secret veins that waved like reeds inside his guts.

[I must cure the White God.]

I went to the woods and there, by the distant noise of the Father's and Yellow Twin's fire-birds, I called on Oshun, the Mother of The Dead, to receive a ghost-slug.

> *'Oshun mori yeye o*
> *alade ko yu oni male*
> *enti ti ti eko ofidere ma oto efun*
> *eni gua ni kado maguemi cobori.'*

That night I found the creature under the moonlight and slipped it inside my pocket.

> *'Mbe, Mbe ma Yeye,*
> *Mbe, Mbe ma Yeye.'*

I sang a thanks-prayer.

'Doctor wants to bite you?' the Yellow Twin asked when she saw me coming out of his room.

'I come to cure him.'

'How?'

[The Yellow Twin is holding four baby moles in her hands. Are they asleep?]

'Need *blanco*, white.'

I remember when it was just us: *Madre*, *Padre*, you, me and *Isla*. Then the painter from the great-land came. He had the sea in his lungs when we found him on the beach. *Padre* sent us to look for *blanco*, to bring Obatala to blow inside the painter's chest.

The Yellow Twin went to the barn and cut the goat's tail. When she gave it to me some of the hairs were still blood-rich, but most had the colour of moon-threads.

'*Blanco*,' she said. I smiled.

We collected fallen feathers from the seagulls. At first

she wanted to throw stones to the birds but I didn't let her.
'Don't want to angry *espíritus*.'
We looked for the pearly stones that slept in the mud. I taught the girl the secret songs we used to awake them.

> *'Obatala Oba tasi Obada badá*
> *badanera ye okulaba okuala*
> *ache olobo ache omo ache ariku baba Ago.'*

In the back yard, we blew inside empty pale snail shells to summon their souls. We stole a pitcher of foaming goat milk while the Cook and the Housekeeper were fucking in the larder.

The doctor sat on the mattress writing. He was wearing many shirts and a blue wool coat. Still he shivered.
'Whitecabbageandbear…Nothingstrange…nothingsurprising… notasinglehint…'
I sat by his side.
'I've a fever… I'm very ill and I don't know why. You should go. Go, you're going to get ill too.' he insisted.
'I am not ill.' I imitated his whispering. Is this a game? 'I stay, doctor.'
'No, go.'
'I'm here. I bring white milk. For you.'
The doctor drowned in sweat and fever-madness. His grey lips kept mumbling the same word.
'Augusta… Augusta… Augusta…'
I stroked his forehead. His cheekbones had grown under the skin.
'Augusta…'
I placed my lips on his lips to silence him, feeling inside me the tremble of doing something forbidden.
[I saw you once kissing the painter, in the purple caves under the cliff. He had been living with us and the *Isla* for seven moons. I know that's why he gave you the gold later,

so we could run away in the boat when mainlanders threw us away from *Isla*.]

I lay sixteen seagulls' feathers around the mattress before undressing him to wash his body with cold milk. Then I placed the ghost-slug on his bare chest. The animal moved slowly, leaving a silver trace. I knew that sooner or later the *abiku* would get curious and would come out to follow that bright path.

> '*Baba eruye Obatala eruye*
> *Obatala eruye aye aye mogue ye*
> *mogua Oggun ache Baba, ache Yeye jakua Babá.*'

Nine days had passed since I freed the white slug in the back yard. I was bringing a clean chamber pot and found the doctor dressed and out of bed. He wandered around the room, but sometimes his hands still searched for support from the table or the carved headboard.

There is only one thing which will nourish the White God. *Padre* taught us that.

'Doctor...'

We were sitting on the bed. I lifted my gown and petticoat to show him my bloodstained shift.

'What—? Have you hurt yourself?'

'You want blood.' I tried to reach his hand.

He crossed his arms. 'No, I don't.'

'Yes, want blood, I know it.'

'I don't— That's insane...' he whispered. He moved back.

'This is me, I want it for you.' I showed him my ankle, then my calf. A single fat drop of *sangre* ran down my leg.

His breath was heavy as the winter's wind. 'No, I thought you meant good. This is no good.' He was smoothing his breeches with his hands.

'For you.'

'Why are you doing this?' He couldn't take his eyes off the drop of blood. 'Why are you doing this to me?'

When he closed his eyes tightly I took his hand and brought it under my shift so he could feel the warmness between my thighs. He shook like a thin tree in a storm.

'This is no good.' The doctor pulled his hand away.

'This is no—'

[I quiet his mouth with my red fingers, fighting the soft barrier of his lips until I feel the moistened tip of his tongue.]

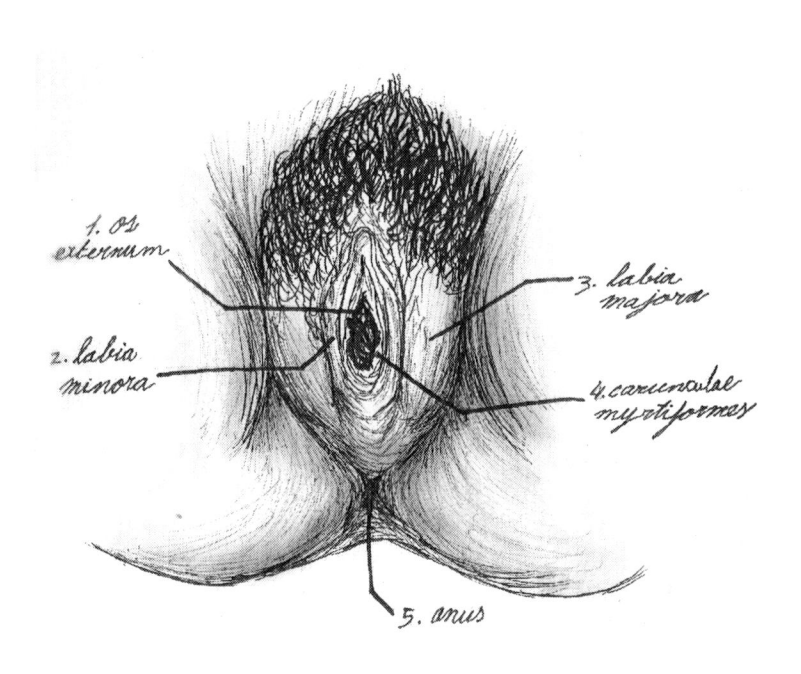

1. os externum
2. labia minora
3. labia majora
4. caruncolae myrtiformes
5. anus

Chapter 7

29th December

I assisted the doctor with the examination of the scullion's body. Turmeric wanted to stay too & finally the doctor let her hold the basin to collect the organs. When the doctor emptied the wet acidic substance in the scullion's stomach, I could not hold back my nausea & had to leave the room. Strong odours affect me during pregnancy.

4th January

The doctor is sick. Last winter, I lost the groom because of the bloody flux. All our cows died & we had to change diet. If the doctor goes, I am losing the most valuable material for my study.

Later. I sent my *dubh* to bring him something healthy to eat—Negroes are not affected by the same illnesses as humans.

12th January

The doctor is still sick. As I supposed, his Norman blood (which comes from a place where the warm climate has turned people into indulgent sheep) lessens the natural strength of his Scotch ancestry. For instance, Miss Bilsland told me the doctor's mother (a French woman) did not survive her first mild winter in

Edinburgh. It seems reasonable to think the Highland winter might also be fatal to her son.

16th January
Cinnamon has cut the goat's tail. He seems to confuse his mating instincts with his predatory ones. I asked *mo duine* to take him when hunting. *Mo duine* says that Cinnamon cannot go because he does not hear the shots. I believe that the extraordinary intelligence of our son makes *mo duine* feel overwrought.

If Cinnamon finds pleasure in cutting things, I will let him help with my dissections.

Later. I cannot find my microscope.

22nd January

I have seen the doctor again for the first time in 4 weeks. He looks smaller & his skin has the colour of dirty snow. I brought him to my studio to examine him but he refused to undress.

I fear his mind might be damaged. His last idea has been banning beer. According to him, it is poisoned & it caused his own illness, the scullion's death & the maid's paralysis. Is all this the product of a vivid imagination? He has read too many of these ridiculous gothic romances —I took his books this morning & burnt them. I also did an exhaustive search among the doctor's belongings. He does not have my microscope.

31st January

I was playing chess with the doctor while he was talking about a very boring subject (the war between England & France) when Cinnamon appeared. My boy immediately noticed the spectacles, they are humiliating as a cane to an old man. Cinnamon possesses an extraordinary sense of sight & touch. For example, he loves playing with the clavichord: he dismantles & assembles it again in less than a day. He touched, licked & tested with great energy the strength of the spectacles. When the doctor tried to find them, Cinnamon hit the doctor's face. The man was surprised, but at last his cheeks & nose displayed some colour. He started laughing, & my boy screamed, as he does to show he is pleased.

Later. The cook to made an inventory of every single tool, object & food item in the kitchen. It took him more than two days, and to prevent him losing concentration on his task, I did not allow him to eat or sleep. My microscope is not there.

2nd February

I followed my *dubh* this morning. When collecting the full chamber pots, she climbed to the doctor's room & looked through the keyhole. When I grasped her arm, her eyes opened wide & her body lost motion: this is known as *prey response*, being natural in herbivore animals. I looked through the keyhole too. The doctor stood naked at the wash basin, rubbing his skin with soap until it turned red.

My *dubh* finds pleasure in observing a male. This implies that she has started feeling the need for mating in the middle of winter. Could her species & the doctor's breed together? I must examine her reproductive organs.

Later. My dubh*'s vagina:*
Absence of the thin membrane that covers the lower part of the *os externum*—it has been perforated & it is not a part of the *Meatus*. It has receded & formed the *carunculae myrtiformes*.

5th February

Mo duine, the doctor, Turmeric & I drank whisky together in the Big Parlour. *Mo duine* is somewhat interested in the doctor's research about that beer disease & congratulated him for taking this drink away from the servants – as if *mo douine* knew about science, or how to read for that matter.

After the first bottle, Turmeric shot her pistol because she said she had seen squirrels in the ceiling. The doctor seemed annoyed by the noise. He choked on a mouthful of whisky.

The second bottle gone, Turmeric fell deeply asleep. *Mo douine* pissed into the chamber pot that is kept under the table, wetting the floor & the doctor's white breeches. The man started swearing. *Mo duine* & I laughed at his delicate French manners.

Later. The housekeeper complains that my *dubh* cannot walk. I had to hit the lazy animal. The cane made her forget the distress she said she felt between her legs.

9th February

~~I like the doctor a lot, he's so dear to me even if we just met a few months ago. Today I'd the most delightful time with him & so delightful all started with me asking why he's always smoking his poppies, I've read that they make one sleepy, so I thought them useless in what concerns to the exercise of the intellectual mind. But he told me that it's the opposite, the white poppies revive the wits so they're for thinkers like him & I, so he prepared them for me. Remembering my *dubh* spying on him, I took *A treatise on the theory & practice of midwifery* & opened it on the second chapter, to show him pictures of the external parts of reproduction in women & I asked, first? & he said, what? & I said, is this the first time doctor? & he said, I've assisted at births & seen the consequences of venereal diseases which turn these pretty things into something you cannot imagine, & are you asking me first? I laughed & said you're a very concerned doctor but I wanted to know... have your hands touched this for something else than a medical purpose? Of course not, as if I had asked him if he drank human blood. The pleasure from the flesh confuses the intellect & makes a man weak. I'm a virgin myself & more than proud to admit it. I inquired about Miss Bilsland but he merely said a strict woman who used to belt my mouth whenever I spoke French — & he was caressing his lips — but precisely because I love her I'd never do to her what animals do to each other. I'd never force her perfect body to undergo the invasive embrace~~

~~of coition, the mutations of pregnancy or the rip of birth, all for the sake of satisfying some vile impulses that I'm perfectly able to control by now.~~

~~How wretched you are, my dear doctor, all about your Miss Bilsland, but she can't bear children, as she's been ill since adolescence. You should accept that, her reproduction instincts suppressed, she's turned into a very boring old lady who is always in the bank, managing numbers, making employees. Do you think she is still a woman?~~

10th February

Reading the last pages of this diary, I have come to the conclusion that poppies inspire nothing but nonsense & distorted feelings. From now on, I shall refrain from indulging.

Later. I discovered the housekeeper lighting one candle in my studio. She said it was for Saint Anthony to find my microscope. I burned her lips with the candle. She must stop talking nonsense.

13th February

The doctor has given Cinnamon & Turmeric a telescope that he acquired when travelling in South America. They have been using it to spy centipedes & spiders on the ceiling. Then Turmeric cut a branch from the Yew in the garden & used it to make the insects fall on the floor. They got 15 spiders and 12 centipedes inside a wooden box. We brought it to my studio so I could choose what specimens were worthy of being in my collection. Turmeric liked an orange centipede. She did not listen when I explained how to use the dissection needles. She broke the creature in half. Cinnamon is more talented. He understands how the pieces work & knows to puncture between the joints. He showed me the biggest spider perfectly opened. The needles had not damaged any of its 8 eyes.

The doctor came when Turmeric was smashing the other spiders with the telescope. He was angry. He did not take the telescope away but the wooden box. He freed the insects in the back yard.

The telescope reminded me of the disappearance of my own microscope. I told the servants they will not eat until they find it.

14th February

Turmeric found the microscope (or what remains of it) in the cellar. No doubt only the primitive mind of my *dubh* could have been capable of desiring such an atrocity. I cannot make her understand what an irreparable damage not only to me but science itself she has caused. I shall think of a way of correcting her behaviour.

15th February

The maid is dying. She has not opened her eyes in days. The doctor finds her pulse too weak. The housekeeper was asking for a priest. This is impossible due to the snow. Yet the woman moaned & tore her hair out until the doctor himself admitted to knowing the Latin service. He has dressed in black & will conduct a ceremony for the ignorant servants.

Later. The doctor's words: In nomine patris et filii et spiritus sancti os frontaleos parietale os nasale os lacrimale virginis mariea joseph et omnium sanctorum lingua cerebrum angelelorum intestinum archangelorum digitus patriarcharum apostolorum oculus virginum sanctorum...

The doctor took water to anoint the maid. When he touched her eyelids she shook & a wail escaped from her grey lips. It was so intense & vibrant that Turmeric ran under the bed, *mo duine* jumped & the servants rushed to the door, screaming like calves being slaughtered. Only my dear Cinnamon remained calm & even giggled a bit. The doctor threw the rest of the water over the woman—I wonder if he did this on purpose or because of the panic. She suffered severe convulsions & fell from the bed. When her body hit the floor, her wailing ceased. She was dead. The cook prayed & the housekeeper yelled to the Lord to take the Devil out of the house. The doctor approached me & whispered a single word: Hydrophobia.

He & *mo duine* took the pistols & ammunition & went out to find the mad dogs.

I have been hearing shots & the wolves howling all night.

Chapter 8

I helped the doctor bury the maid beside the lake.

'Here, it's beautiful,' he said. Snowflakes speckled his black hair like stars in the midnight sky.

'But—' I clung to the doctor's arm,'—need trees on her, trees are good, they are old *espíritus*. They will clean her *espíritu*—'

'Spectres... Nonsense.'

I chose a place under the trees while he tied his horse to a burned trunk. He had been keeping from me since his illness. Although I cured him with my blood he's angry, probably because he knew about my deal with the *abiku* in the Mother's belly. *Padre* advised us that Obatala, the One Who Watches For All, wouldn't approve such things. [But the house is swallowing me, *Hermano*, and I can only pray to the *abiku* now. *Oscuridad*. The shadows.]

I dug carefully to plant the branch of bourtree that the Housekeeper had given us to chase the Devil away. The doctor hit the green roots with the shovel.

'You're hurting them,' I told him.

He stopped, white-air puffing from his mouth.

'Are alive,' I explained, but he turned his head to the bundle wrapped with a blanket on the horse's back and did not answer.

I was in the kitchen, cleaning a crust of dried gruel from the big pot. The Yellow Twin had a sore throat and a bit of fever, so the doctor had prescribed her sticky oats. Oats were *blanco*, and *blanco* was good to heal. I didn't hear the Mother approaching. She grabbed my arm and dragged me up the main stairs. The Mother only entered the kitchen when there was trouble. The house watched us all the time but she was the one in charge when there was big trouble.

The house was the eyes, she was the claws.

She was taking me to her special room she called her study.

'Mistress, I'm begging you...' I remembered the maid saying this when she was about to get the cane. 'Mistress please don't hurt me I'm begging you, Mistress I'll be good, I'll be good, swear to God, Mistress...'

She didn't look at me.

The midday light entered through the dirty study windows, making ghost-shapes in the jars where mutilated creatures swam sleeping. It touched the hungry tools waiting in the shelves, and made the laughing skulls on the table whiter. The doctor was here too. I could still be saved.

She made me stay upright in front of the table.

'What is this?' she asked me.

I looked at the metal pieces, wood splinters and bits of glass.

'What—is—this?'

I recognised the creature the Brown Twin attacked. Is it dead? Must be. The Mother seemed angry, much more than when she was in front of the maid's corpse.

'Doctor— See? She cannot understand. She has these language problems, I think it might be related to her vocal apparatus and I was already carrying some tests but...'

The Mother was talking but my eye kept focused on the cane, that awaited for me on the table like a snake.

'I cannot get a new one in winter...'

The Mother.

The doctor fingers' were interlaced.

['*Por favor...* please...' I whisper.].

'She destroyed it and I've to punish her. I suppose you also tamed that horse of yours?'

I kept looking at the doctor, who swayed back and forth

while he looked through the window.

['Please...' I beg him.]

The Mother took a little metal piece and handed it to me. 'Swallow'.

I didn't move.

She took the cane and hit my breast. My knees trembled when she dragged me to the chair and pain filled my limbs when I twisted and twisted trying to escape. She tied my wrists to the armrests.

[¿*Por qué?* Why is she punishing me?]

'Help me here,' The Mother said, and the doctor answered something that I couldn't understand. My eye was water. She was pressing the metal piece to my lips.

'Swallow.'

I kicked the floor and tried to rise from the chair. My nails scratched the wood and my teeth pressed together so hard that I felt as if my head was being smashed by the beak of some giant bird.

'Swallow.'

She hit my fingers with the cane and I saw yellow and purple and my mouth opened and a scream broke free—

'Shhh...'

She put the metal piece inside my mouth. It went down—I coughed—I wanted to spit it out—she pressed my nose and my mouth with her hands—the cough got stuck in my throat—my eyes were like the sea—my arms and legs shook—my chest creaked.

When she eased the pressure on my nose I breathed and knew I had swallowed it.

'Good.' She had another piece. 'Open.'

Tears streamed from my eye while I closed my teeth tighter. She smiled.

Obatala dibeniwua binike...

The doctor was behind her and he was not looking at the window any more, just at my eye.

'She's not an animal.' He held the Mother's arm.

'What? Get away from me. I'm teaching her.'

'You're torturing her, stop—'

She pushed him away. 'I'm sick of your sensitivity, doctor.' She brandished the cane at him. 'Shall I tell Miss Bilsland about your peculiar interest in my servant?'

He covered his face when she hit him.

'I am sure she'll find it... amusing.'

The doctor left the room. He was gone. I was lost. I felt I was swimming in cold mud.

[I am drowning.]

'Open.'

I closed my body like a hedgehog.

'Open.'

The cane hissed. The piece of glass she was holding in the other hand shone like the moon.

I was locked in the cellar alone.

[I try to vomit but I can't
see
if
all the pieces come
out
of my body.

My stomach burns and my eye is dry. The smell of my own vomit makes me feel faint.

The *abiku*'s milky hands,

I feel them

cold and sticky over my forehead.

'Abiku, *te necesito, te necesito.* Abiku *por favor, te necesito. Ven,* abiku, *ven, te necesito, ven,* abiku *ven te necesito,* abiku, abiku.'

I need to find a way out, but
my body is

poisoned and
won't
obey.
Oscuridad.
Make the Mother die *abiku* make the Mother die rip her belly from the inside and make her die I don't want to die I want to
pray.
My throat swells and my guts yell.
I cry.
The blood in my mouth
 is going to drown me
I howl.
I lick the walls to get rid of it but there's always more coming from inside me.
I must have the cursed kitten in my stomach,
scratching with his paws
trying to get out.
I rip my my shift.

'Sal, sal, sal.'

I scrub my belly with stones and dirt from the ground.
The *abiku* has to get out.
The *abiku* has to get out.
The *abiku* has to get out or
it'll eat
my
heart.
I scream until my mouth is so full of fluid I cannot breathe so I swallow it and when I do my stomach cringes and I retch more

blood.

'Madre, madre…'
I don't want our dark *Padre* but our white *Madre* here.

I beg for our mother to come from the realm of dead. I
call her because she brought me to this world
and this world is killing me.
'*Madre, madre, madre, madre, madre, madre, madre...*'
My voice fades but I keep mouthing the words because if I stop

I'll die.

A heavy noise.
'*Madre...*'
'I'm here, my child.'

'*Madre...*'
'I'm here, my child.'
Is that light? My eye hurt.
'*Madre...*'
'I'm here, my child, I'm here...'
A shadow fell over me while I sank in the arms of a warm body.]

The doctor held me in the cellar and made me eat soft bread—as if I was a baby bird, he chewed it before pushing it in my mouth.
'Eat, eat... it'll help you.'
In the dying candlelight, his eyes were invisible, but his smell, oily hair and soap scented sweat, comforted me. He cleaned the blood and crumbs from my mouth with his fingers.
'You'll be all right.'
He licked his fingers.
'I'm afraid.' I grabbed his hand tighter. '*Dime algo, por favor...* Tell something, *dime algo...*'
'What can I say? What can I—'
He pressed his cold cheek towards my hand.
'*Je me rends.*'

Chapter 9

Glenfinnan, Saturday Feb. 21 1804

Dear Dr Jenner,

I hope you will excuse the liberty I have taken in writing these few lines. I hope they will find you in good health as they leave me at present, thanks be to God. Please, I beg you, do not put these pages to what you might consider a better use—feeding the fire, for instance, as we are now in the cruellest point of winter. I know I am neither your apprentice nor your colleague, not even your dear son—as you used to address me when I was a brat of ten years old fetching cuckoo's eggs to assist you with your experiments. But I am deeply concerned about the future of a certain family—the McTavish family—& I shall beg my mentor—not only an excellent & compassionate doctor but also a man of God—to advise me in this matter.

Six years have passed since I, in accordance with your wishes, disappeared from your life. Nevertheless, I have been following your advances, and read **An Inquiry into the Causes and Effects of the Variolae Vaccinae** as soon as it was published by Sampson's—and I almost wrote then to congratulate you on such a masterful work. Controversy has arisen, but I firmly believe that time will support your ideas &, eventually, allocate to you the place you deserve—that of the righteous amongst the great names of science.

I was only a little disappointed to discover that

although you mentioned all sort of cases—like James Phipps or Sarah Portlock—you omitted the first person who underwent the inoculation of Cow Pox & the variolation of Small Pox without harm. You called me a fool when I did this to myself eight years ago & now here we are, sir, you have our wonderful discovery published & I have been banished not only from authorship but even as a case—as the first case. Miss Bilsland mentioned in her last letter that you have been invited to the court of King George, and perhaps I should not be surprised by my neglect. Why would you remember this uncultured Scottish doctor that accompanied you everywhere a few years back when you have the King for company?

You may be pleased to hear that I have changed & now pray for the redemption of my miserable soul. After I left your side in 1797, I sailed around the world as the personal physician of one Captain Langley. Although you, who refused the invitation of the great Captain Cook, had tried to dissuade me from this idea many times, I have to say I found the experience quite pleasant—apart from sea sickness & mutinies. When we were crossing the Atlantic, I prevented a dramatic spread of Smallpox by vaccinating the crew—a few losses & some amputations were the only consequences. I also used our—I believe I may so call it—vaccine with the people I met in the islands, as indeed they are the most powerless in facing what for them is a curse sent by raging gods. In my spare time, I amused myself with our old experiment of using human blood as a manure, since in Central America I discovered plants that feed on all sort of things—like insects—to survive.

In 1801, when I was sailing South America's coast, news of the decline in Miss Bilsland's health reached me & I at once took a ship to return to Scotland. I realised then that I love her more than my life & the entire world with all its wonders. Inspired by one of your most brilliant articles—**Essay on Marriage**—I decided that my feelings deserved to be sacred before the eyes of God, so I proposed to her. With her Consumption almost cured—thanks to my care, I shall say—we are to marry this Summer of 1804 & perhaps next spring I will be holding an infant. You & Mrs Jenner could bring kind Ned, pretty Catherine & little Robert for dinner on St. Andrew's day.

But now I must turn to the fundamental reason I write to you. I am in the Highlands, where Mrs McTavish—a close friend of our family—is pregnant & requires the attention of a doctor during the winter. This good lady is a very gentle & merciful mother—she already has two heavenly infants.

Something terrible is happening here & I want to implore your help. Due to wild dogs that wander through these mountains, Hydrophobia has entered the house & is spreading in a deadly rush. Two healthy youngsters have died & one of the McTavish's children is severely ill. I am treating her with **allium sativum**—this & the poppy alleviate the pain & fever. However, as you know, Hydrophobia cannot be cured & humans who contract it are more miserable than dogs—as they cannot without sin be put out of their misery.

Impotence & curiosity have led me to the most unexpected discovery & you are the very first person to *read about it. I have strong reasons to believe that I also contracted Hydrophobia during my stay here but I survived its symptoms. Here I send you the records:*

30th December
— infected through the blood of a dead boy.

2nd January
— headache, anxiety, hallucinations.

4th January
— vomiting, fever, hallucinations.

7th January
— sweating, fever, uncontrollable shaking of the limbs.

8th-16th January
— I cannot recall these days. Paralysis & fever — I believe.

17th January
— motion recovered, fever drops, eating & drinking in small quantities.

20th January
— out of bed.

22nd January
— recovery.

My disease began with the most extraordinary cause——it was not a bite but the merest contact with contaminated blood from a scullion boy. Three days after, the illness followed a period of exactly eight & twenty days. You will notice I did not experience fear of water or foaming, but the rest—fever, vomiting, paralysis, anxiety & hallucinations—are symptoms I have observed in the others.

Thus it seems Hydrophobia transmitted through blood provokes a less fatal version of the disease. To prove my statement, Mr McTavish—who shares my interest in the animal world—helped me hunt a mad dog. I let it bite me & although the injuries are painful, after six days they have started to heal—I enclose some drawings of their development.

I find it very likely that my own immunity can heal this disease, in the same way we discovered that fluids contained in Smallpox blisters can be inoculated in healthy patients to save them from this distemper.

I realise I am being wicked & selfish, taking a pen to write to the one I betrayed. But we developed together the first vaccine against Smallpox & now, by applying a similar principle, we could study a vaccine against Hydrophobia too. Imagine the vaccination being proved as a miraculous device in the eyes of the sceptics once again. You would be the most respectable doctor in Britain & I—your assistant—would find the strength to ask your forgiveness one more time.

I will now take my horse & fight against snow, wind & cold to bring this letter to Duncasburgh to make sure you receive it. I will pray to God every day until we are blessed with your presence in the Highlands.

With my best wishes to my dear mentor I am
Your faithful & obedient servant
Dr Charles Bilsland, MD

PS—If you would be so gracious as to assist me with these necessities I would be eternally grateful, as I have inoculation lancets & a scarificator, but recently was deprived of the microscope. I am also in great need of turpeth mineral—**hydrargyri sulphas flava**—which has been used against Hydrophobia in dogs & I would happily test with my human patients.

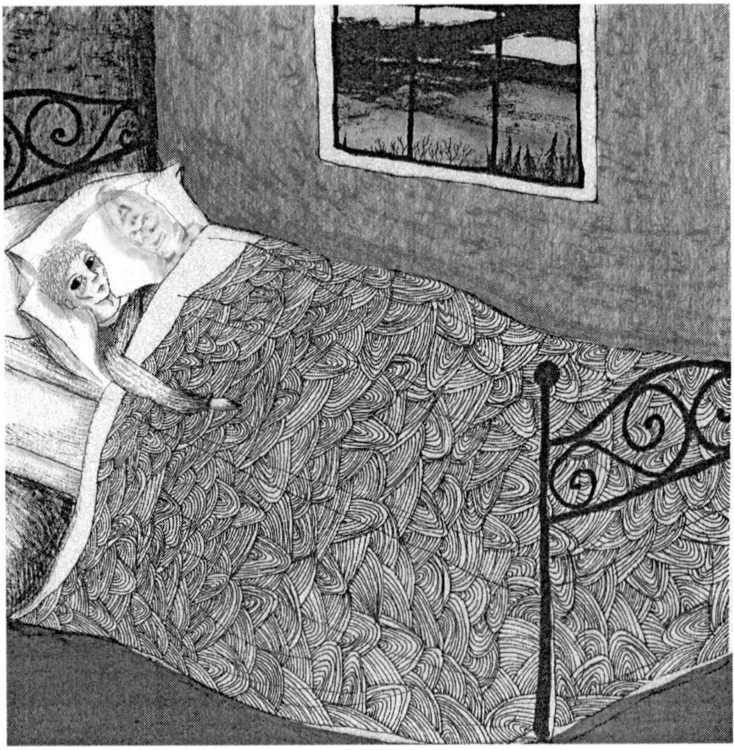

Chapter 10

'What's she doing here?' the Mother said, entering her bedchamber.

'Assisting me,' the doctor replied, without getting up from the chair beside the bed where the Yellow Twin slept. The Father stood silent by the iron headboard.

'Come, *dubh*.'

The Mother's words dragged me to her. I still felt the sores from the glass and metal and pain in my mouth.

'I need her to clean my tools, to—' the doctor said. The Mother clenched my shoulder. '*Dubh*, come here.'

'Your child is ill, she needs a doctor. I need an assistant. No assistant... no doctor.' The doctor opened his case and started collecting his bright tools.

'How dare you?' You fool, Miss Bilsland—!' the Mother shouted at him and I could feel the *abiku*'s little fingers pushing my back from inside the Mother's big belly.

'Is *she* going to cure your children?' the doctor said, spitting to clean one of his knives. 'Come here,' he called to me.

A rush of icy wind opened the window. Everyone turned to observe the night. Lightning. I'm sure I was the only one seeing the *abiku* running under the bed. I could sense its purple nostrils trembling with pleasure while it inhaled the Yellow Twin's pain. The Father closed the window, and spoke for the first time, his red eyes glaring.

'We need him.'

The Mother glanced at her daughter, whose skin was powdery, as if covered by ashes. Her body, buried under heavy sheets, seemed like the corpse of a baby.

'Take your pet, doctor'

The Mother hit my head before letting me go.

The Father left the room, saying he was going to hunt. The Yellow Twin's eyes were sunken in black, her hands, rigid and thin, had the cold mole-fingers. The Mother freshened her forehead with a wet cloth. Her body shook and the doctor forced her to sit. He lighted his pipe while she looked at it as if it was a goldenrod fat worm sliding from his mouth.

'It's good for you,' he said after tasting it.

'My child... don't let her touch my child...' The Mother stared at me. She had not realised yet that the *abiku* wanted to take her daughter. Probably she didn't even know that the weight she felt inside her body was from her baby's corpse. The *abiku* must have eaten the baby long time ago, leaving just the tiny bones to play with when it was bored.

'I'll do everything to cure her. But you have to rest.'

The doctor placed his pipe in the Mother's hands.

'Don't let...'

'You need this. Yes. Good, good.'

He helped her to hold it until she started taking small sips.

'Good.'

The Mother and the pipe were sleeping. I held the teapot while the doctor gave willow-bark tea to the Yellow Twin. The blanket drank most of it. The sun was going down. My teeth chattered when I was not standing on the orange glow on the floor left by the brightness of the fireplace.

The Yellow Twin's hair was warm like the doctor when the *abiku* was eating him. I had saved him with my magic, and I could have saved the Yellow Twin too. I didn't want to feel her wet cheeks when she watched the sparkling, faceless *abiku* bending over her. I didn't want to listen to her screams when the *abiku* inserted its dog-teeth behind her knees where the flesh was soft. I didn't want to smell her heart rotting when the *abiku* started dissolving it with its saliva. I didn't want to see the fleshy inside of her small bones after the *abiku* had cracked them.

[I want to save the Yellow Twin.

But you know I won't do it.

I want to punish the Mother.]

I touched the white ribbon that tied the doctor's hair. He shivered and turned to look at me. It seemed he was going to smile, but his lips just let some words out.

'Going to make more tea. Keep soaking it and padding her forehead.'

He handed me the wet cloth and left.

I held it, letting drops fall on the floor one by one by one. The Twins have always reminded me of the Ibiji, twin sons of the Warrior God Shangó, who came to Earth to torment humans. They had fun causing troubles, arguments, wars. They also possessed fire birds, like the ones the Yellow Twin and the Father used to summon *sangre*. In the forest I always ran away from the *bangs*, knowing that if they spotted me between the branches they would—

The wind was striking the window. The Yellow Twin sat up on the bed and gave a rough fear-cry.

The Ibiji's eyes had turned raven black, and her mouth was full of saliva. I stepped back, holding the wet cloth tighter. Water could protect me, I'd learned that from the scullion.

> '*Obatala dibeniwa binike*
> *ala lo laa ache afizu Ocha ailala*
> *abi koko alaru mati la Ayuba ago*'

'Where's the girl?'

The doctor was back.

'She go— she's hunted'

I was still holding the cloth so hard that my palm hurt.

'Damn it… I have to find her.'

He took the candlestick.

'Go with you?' I asked.

'No—' He looked at the Mother, who hadn't woken up yet. 'Very well,' he said, placing my hand on his arm, 'don't let her bite you.'

In the Twins' room the curtains danced slowly. I looked down to see a copper cockroach running from the light to hide in a pillow on the floor. There was a black horse trying to run, his whinny like wood cracking. His legs had been nailed to the wood, so his gallop would never take him out of the room. Damned-tree-horse. Is his *espíritu* also raging for revenge?

The Father sat in one of the beds, and he was whining while he kissed a bottle.

We took the big stairs down.

[I think about *Madre* running away from her house in the Mainland with *Padre*. They sailed away in a boat as small as a nut-shell, she holding you in her arms, small and precious, like a pearl. *Padre* invoked the goddess Oshun so that the sea would take you all to an invisible island nobody else knew about. *Isla*.]

The empty bedchamber on the first floor was covered with dust and broken furniture rotting. The window showed two ghosts that looked like us and I dreamed the *nieve* outside, snowflakes licking the windowsill.

I stayed at the edge of the room when the doctor entered the Mother's study. No place was dark enough for the White God.

We kept on through the small dining room to the Blue Parlour, where the Mother kept her music box, a golden goat of thin legs, and in the corner a man's head with the whitest skin I'd ever seen. He had holes instead of eyes. He had lost them like I lost my one . Who kept it? *Mi ojo*. My eye. Someone took my *ojo* to see the things I see. Or for me to forget what I saw then.

We entered the Big Parlour where the empty chairs were the only guests. The Brown Twin played under the table, using a fork to poke a doll dressed in a tartan nightgown. The fireplace was lit and I saw the *abiku* dancing with sombre *espíritus* on the walls, calling the Brown Twin to join. But he couldn't hear them.

We took the servants' stairs. The candle in the doctor's hand was dripping. He held it away from me, and muttered.

I tried to take the candlestick. He shook his head. I saw the red spots in his the shirt sleeve. [Is the house biting him too?]

The ceiling trembled. The Mother? A yell came from the kitchen. We both ran down the stairs.

The Housekeeper, holding a pan, screamed, and the Cook's hands were covered with blood. The Brown Twin cowered on the floor, too close to the burning oven. If he moved to the right, the jumping flames would nibble at him. They all stared at the Ibiji, whose mouth was foaming with pink.

The doctor gave me the candlestick.

'Everyone... don't move...' he said while he approached the Ibiji. 'Easy... easy...' the doctor went on, but the Ibiji ran towards the Brown Twin, who was so scared that he stepped back and touched the oven. A yell, a smell, fired-meat. The doctor held the Ibiji from behind, they fought, the Ibiji tried to bite him but the doctor grabbed her jaw. The Ibiji fell on the floor shaking and howling (like the scullion, like the maid).

'*Bhampair, bhampair...*' the Housekeeper screeched.

'My child...'

The Mother entered the room, but before she could get to the Ibiji the doctor restrained her.

'Can't touch her—' the doctor said.

'My chid, my child...'

The Mother's eyes grew wide and her mouth opened

wide, so wide it was going to cut her face in two. I could see the *abiku*'s gleaming fingers under her tongue.

'She's infected...' The doctor kept talking but the Mother grunted like a mad boar and I could feel how the *abiku* inside her fought back—but the doctor was stronger.

The Ibiji screamed on the floor, calling the *abiku*.

The Housekeeper screamed *bhampair*.

The cook screamed without words, looking at his hands.

The Mother screamed *my child*.

The Brown Twin screamed death, looking at his burned arm.

Someone pushed me and the candlestick fell.

Oscuridad.

The Father sped to the doctor and broke the bottle over his head.

[I scream.]

Chapter 11

23th February

My daughter has

24th February

~~My~~

Cinnamon cried all night. His burned arm deprives him of rest. I took him to my bed to comfort him.
The doctor prescribed poppy wine: 3 glasses a day in small sips.

The doctor is not as nauseated as yesterday, although he still moves with remarkable difficulty—even if he was trying to protect me, *mo duine* should not have used the kitchen stool after the whisky bottle broke.

Later. My murdered siblings were always alive in my mother's words. After 1746, she composed poems to mourn our family every day we spent hidden in this same house. She used to say that the lions pulled her teeth & devoured her children raw.

Where are the lions now? If only I could grab them to make them burst into blood & torment.

25th February

The doctor maintains it was Hydrophobia. I have not detected any canine bite in Turmeric's alabaster skin. But there is something inside her body which has killed her. An incorporeal creature? A poison? I have to lift her skin to inspect every organ until I find it.

Later. The doctor needs a cold, dark place so I have given him the cellar. He asserts that, in my state, I should not be present. What he calls *my state* is nothing but the earnest desire to find the truth, as a scientist. My pregnancy is just my privilege as a woman.

26th February

In the cellar, the food jars have been put aside. The holes to store the barrels of whisky are filled with snow. Candles illuminate the green veins under my child's skin. She was wearing only her nightgown. I went upstairs & brought a blanket.

Later. We put on the aprons & tied handkerchieves soaked with mint around our noses. We undressed Turmeric. I made sure her feet remained covered with the blanket. The doctor grabbed the incision knife, but I stopped him. I wanted to do it. He questioned my abilities. I am the mother, what else is required?

When the doctor was using the double saw to section the ribs, I retched. I could not stand the sound, like a dried trunk being axed. He handed me the basin where he was leaving the dirty tools, holding my forehead while I vomited. Seeing I could not breathe, he took me out from the cellar. He tried to open the house's main doors to bring me outside, but they were blocked by the snow. He opened the windows from the main parlour instead & made me sit next to them. Everything was white except the sky, which had a treacherous grey hue. I felt as if a scalpel was puncturing my lungs. I remembered Mother's song:

> *O, chì, chì mi na mòrbheanna;*
> *O, chì, chì mi na coireachan,*
> *Chì mi na sgoran fo cheò.*

> *Chì mi gun dàil an t-àite 'san d' rugadh mi;*
> *Cuirear orm fàilte 'sa chànan a thuigeas mi;*
> *Gheibh mi ann aoidh agus gràdh nuair ruigeam,*
> *Nach reicinn air thunnachan òir.*

> *Chì mi ann coilltean; chi mi ann doireachan;*
> *Chì mi ann màghan bàna is toraiche;*
> *Chì mi na fèidh air làr nan coireachan,*
> *Falaicht' an trusgan de cheò.*

The doctor sang along. I was not aware of his knowledge of our language. He placed his arm over my shoulders. I retched on him.

Looking at the basin, blood mixed with vomit, tools floating as dead seagulls on the lake, an idea came to my mind. I asked the doctor. He said no. I asked him again. He did not answer.

Later. It took me hours of persistence but we are to do it promptly.

> *Post-mortem examination.*
> Sectio cadaveris 56 hours after death.
> Head
> Scalp
> Calvarium

>Meninges
>Medullari Substance.
>Chest
>Pleural Cavities
>Pericardium
>Lungs
>Heart.
>Abdomen
>Peritoneal Cavity
>Solid Viscera – Liver, Spleen, Kidneys.
>Hollow Viscera – Stomach, Large Intestine,
>Small Intestine.
>Blood – In veins & Heart.
>Urine – In Bladder.

No anomaly detected.

27th February

> *Hunterian solution*
> Oil of turpentine 5 pt.
> Venice turpentine 1 pt.
> Oil of lavender 2 oz.
> Oil of rosemary 2 oz.
> Vermillion.

We have to wait one day.

The twins sleep. One in the cellar, the other in my bed.

28th February

I went to the kitchen to have the lime water prepared. I ordered the housekeeper (who has lost most of her hair) to change her apron, dirty with blood & grease stains. She did not stop murmuring *bhampair, bhampair...* When I demanded to know where the cook was, she said something about him being too warm. I decided to prepare the lime water myself & sent her to pray because I could not tolerate her smell.

Lime Water

Infuse 1 lb of lime in 6 qt of spring water for 24 hours.

Strain & keep it for use.

29th February

Not even the scented burning of the candles can cover the smell of lemons & cinnamon in the cellar. Pieces, soaked in lime water, are hanging on ropes all over the room. Blood & bile rotted on the floor—I had it cleaned with snow & soap. The doctor was exhausted & begged me for a rest. I ordered the housekeeper & my *dubh* to bring him one of the stuffed chairs from the main parlour.

Later. We do not have enough cinnamon. I am substituting ginger. My *dubh* is out bringing more buckets of snow.

1st March

The pieces have dried & their colour has changed from grey to dark black & finally chestnut. We applied beeswax. I brought my own twine, the same I used for sewing my children's nightgowns.

The doctor has performed a splendid work.

Later. Tonight the housekeeper burst into my chamber crying that a black *bhampair* was attacking the doctor. To end her nightmare, I slapped her face twice. I will punish her if she persists with her pagan obsessions.

2nd March

Still waiting.

I should record a curious fact for my treatise. Last night, I went to the doctor's room to discover what had unhinged the housekeeper. The door was partially open so I could see the chamber invaded by an intoxicating golden mist & the sickly smell of rotten flowers. The doctor lay on the floor, naked to the waist. Sheets were disposed about him in the most particular way, twisted & forming a circle. When my *dubh* bent over him to lick the peach-yellow festering wounds on his arm, he simply turned his head to exhale the poppies. His eyes were like polished jet; his mind was not in the room at all.

My *dubh*'s licking seems to be a mating ritual (common in many mammals) to stimulate the male's reproductive instinct, although she was having little success. This indifference must be another consequence of his Norman blood, which corrupts not only his physical strength but also his sexual maturity. To verify this, an examination of his sexual apparatus is needed.

I am considering inducing coition, so that I

can conduct further research on an experiment performed by Doctor Jenner. He studied the sexual intercourse between a terrier bitch & a fox, giving detailed accounts of three copulations in the same day & the absence of pregnancy after these. The breeding between different species is a mystery I am to solve soon.

Later. Poppies anaesthetise the doctor's virility. I must dispose of them.

3rd March

Following the doctor's instructions, I brought my daughter to the bullseye chamber on the third floor—the warmest place in the mansion. She rests on an armchair covered by plaster of Paris. Her curly hair reminds me of autumn leaves. Her cheeks are like embers. Her lashes are snowy. Her nose & lips pitch black. I imagine her blue eyes behind the grey eyelids despite the fact they are gone (I extracted them myself). The tips of her fingers exhibit a yellowish green. The skin on her arms & legs is ochre with patches of pink. The scent of rotten lemons & cinnamon prevails in the air.

    I will bring *mo duine* & Cinnamon to visit her. They will be very pleased. I will allow *mo duine* to bring the pistols if he promises not to fire them inside the chamber. He will probably want Turmeric to go outside, but I shall not allow it. It is too cold & she needs to rest on her plaster of Paris.
    Drying.
    Dreaming?

Chapter 12

The Woman wanders through the woods. Voiceless, vermillion-feather creatures gazes at her. Animals dreams in cradles of purple moss. When she approaches them...

The sky cried red, the lake welcomed *oscuridad*. I prayed to Oshun, the Mother of the Fish. The moon watched me, round as a pregnant belly, sparkling with expectation. I wandered through the water collecting the yellow flowers that floated erected over Oshun's fluids. I tasted them and squeezed their milk over my breasts. *Blanco*. My shift was embellished with sugary frost. *Oshun mori yeye o.* I soothed the ardour of my secret parts with a pale candle. When my pleasure was bright as the moonlight reflected in the water, I cracked an egg. Its whiteness melted in the black waves.

[The Hare is on the moon tonight.]

The Woman discovers they are nothing but empty carcasses, dried skins, hollow limbs, bloodless hearts...

I walked through the house, dressed in the maid's laced shift. No one wanted it after she died. I liked how it danced over my ankles like sea foam. I caught a glimpse of the Mother's bedchamber, where they all rested. Can you guess what I just did, *Hermano*?

I poured it into the whisky bottle that the Father embraced as he reclined on the helpless wooden horse that galloped nowhere.

I poured it into the cracked tea cups on the bed where the Mother and the Yellow Twin lay. Her arms were the nest for her daughter's empty face sea-green as a raven's egg.

I poured it into the medicine spoon the Brown Twin

drank every day to heal his burnt arm. He snored, hidden under the bed, as warm and blind as when he was inside the Mother's womb.

I poured it into the vase full of rotten flowers, so they could not see me and wake up the Mother.

Magic poppy wine.

...The Woman saw a moonglow behind the spiderweb of branches. It was no other than Obatala who...

The doctor was in the Mother's study, searching through shining little bottles and needles. He must have been looking for the *abiku*, thinking perhaps it was drinking the cursed water the Mother used to fill her jars, or that it swam inside the darkness of the skull's eye sockets.

The doctor was blue-white like the moon, and I was dark as the night sky.

[*Madre* was white and *Padre* was dark. Do you think that means something? With Oshun's help, I am also transforming the house into a drifting island.]

The *nieve* darted behind the window.

'Go, I'm busy,' he said. '...poppies... where...?'

The doctor's hands trembled like his voice. On the large table the skulls were snowdrops on March grass.

'I need my damn poppies...' The doctor grasped a horned head and threw it on the floor, where it splintered. As he reached to take the next skull, I grabbed his hand.

'What?' he asked, pushing me away.'Everything is dead here.'

The skull flew past me, its long fangs flashing, and behind me there was a crack like the sound of lightning.

'Soon there'll be new ones for the collection,' the doctor muttered as he stepped back, throwing twin craniums against the wall.

I walked towards him.

'You could be the next one.' He said, punching a pile of dead and dusty books. They fell to the ground and the dust jumped, hanging like tiny mosquitoes in the air.

I stepped over the mess on the floor.

'I cannot save you.'

The shelves at the doctor's back, full of the wet creatures the Mother keeps in jars, stopped him.

I was so close that his breath warmed my frosted cheeks.

Snowflakes collided behind the window.

I untied my shift's ribbons.

He grabbed a silver jaw the Mother used to cut bones and shells.

My shift fell to my feet, as if I was casting off my own shadow.

Metal fangs glittered under the candlelight, devouring the distance between my body and his.

Te necesito.

I buried my nose in the rough fabric of his shirt, feeling the chill of his waistcoat's silver buttons in my nipples. I sat on the table and then knelt there to place my arms around his neck. My hair waved under his gasps. I tried to taste his mouth, but he groaned and turned his face away from me, hiding in the *oscuridad*. His neck was offered, so I drank from the waterfall of blue veins. Wet, wet, wet. I looked down. He pressed the silver jaw so hard that the fangs tore his skin.

I took his hands. The metal teeth fell.

'Please…' he mumbled when I started licking. 'Please don't…'

I drove his bloody hands all over my body until I was blessed in crimson. Lust bit inside when I brought them between my legs. I moved my hips forwards and backwards, forwards and backwards.

He grabbed my shoulders and I would have fallen if

he had let me go. He hurled me into the Mother's desk. Everything was thrown aside: the hungry metal tools, the hissing cane, the feathered notebooks, the smelly animal skins. Jars exploded in alcoholic sparks when they met the floor. The *espíritus* of haunted creatures raced free through the air. He was over me, licking blood off my face, my neck, my breasts, my belly. He was between my legs licking my thighs. His tongue was inside. I grabbed the skeleton that hanged on the wall and pulled it. A rain of dried bones fell all over my wet body. *Blanco*. I rose to embrace the doctor and taste that shiny redness in his lips. *Rojo*. He pushed me aside.

We rolled on the large table. I needed to feel his skin on my skin, like cool *nieve* over a burning wound. His hair covered my face and tasted sour. I took his waistcoat off to smell his scent: *canela*, alcohol, poppies, mint, rancid soap, sweat and blood. His long fingers were into my mouth, the twin bones of his hips pressed my eager belly. I brushed my lips against the fresh scars on his arms. When I unbuttoned his breeches, his face turned the colour of a dying twilight sun. The windows trembled under the *nieve*'s rage when he rose and I sat on his hips. He was still looking me in the eye when I opened myself to take him.

[My fingers mould the pain into pleasure.]

'*Por favor, por favor...*'

[The *oscuridad* bursts in red.

And violet.

And white.

    My mind is clear, beyond suffering and brightness.

Rojo, violeta, blanco.

I just want to touch it.

To grasp it.

To clutch it.

Liebre, luna.

I am holding it.

I am burning in it.
La liebre, la luna.
The Hare is dancing on the moon. The moon is on fire.]

…Obatala held a hare in his hands and sucked its blood. This was his desire and privilege. The Woman understood it but…

[I am there. I am the Hare.]

'*Dios…*'
　I felt as if this was the first time my soul took my body.
　He was still looking at me, clenching his jaw. His elbows trembled and the *blanco* in his eyes fluttered. He was not there. Yet. I moved my hips.
　'Don't…' He was begging me. 'Don't…'
　I kept moving.
　His voice turned into a soft dog-whimper. His forehead rested on my forehead.
　He looked down when I felt him in my guts, his bones were islands on a frozen sea. He was wet and warm, like a summer's storm.

…Obatala rose his coal eyes and looked inside the Woman's soul and his voice thundered: 'You have seen what no creature must see, so I shall curse you…

'*Obatala… ven, ven conmigo.*'
　'*Je me rappelle de cette journé… la pluie …*'
　Slowly. Our bonded bodies were like two flint rocks. Every tiny movement threatened to bring a blaze. His lips. My hips. He closed his eyes. He pressed his lips onto mine. Soft. Dry. Just once. He tasted like *sangre*.

…every month you will offer me your own blood, and you will feed me with it until I bless your belly on the Hare's

moon.

He kissed me. The silver circles pressed my eyelid. His timid tongue. He didn't open his eyes anymore. Wetness. His fingers brushing under the bandage that covers my *cicatriz* as if he was caressing flesh-coloured poppy's petals. He kissed me. He was in the *oscuridad* now.
  With me.

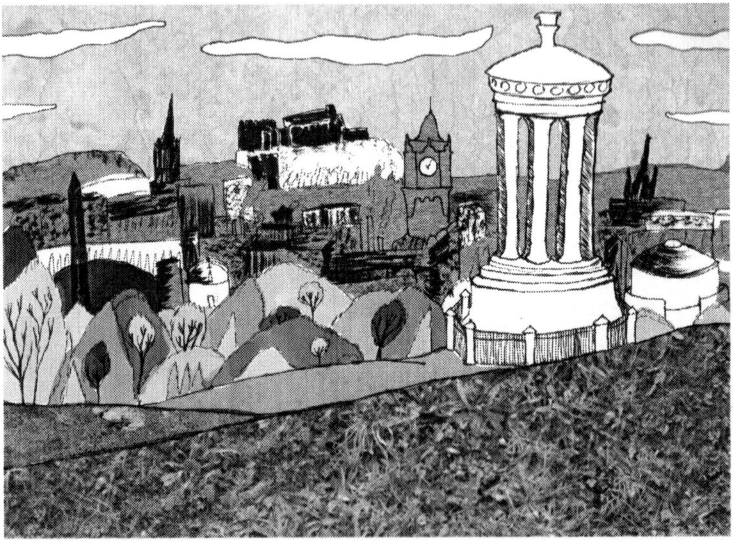

Chapter 13

Glenfinnan, Wednesday March 6th 1804

My dear,

I have not written you in quite a long time—you thought my last letter 'disturbing' & 'irrational'. This morning I rushed to the stables in fear that my poor Seagull had not endured last night's snowstorm. His mane was frozen, but his almond eyes greeted me, pleased to see his master. I rode him around the woods. Everything was blank, meaningless, as those seconds just after a song has died in the air.

& what a raw blue sky.

Do you remember how you mocked my poems, that I sent you from London? Crumpled papers stained with blood that I scribbled on the operating table at St George's Hospital. There will be no metaphors in this letter, no allegories or similar artifices, only the raw truth about your cousin's miserable soul, which started to fall into corruption the very first time he confronted the Highlands & the rain threatened to dissolve his rational mind. She was there, an ebony body that does not belong to this land where sun is so scarce. You told me about her in Edinburgh, a mysterious, fascinating servant, exotic & lacquered as a scorpion.

That first time I met her—she was breathing her own

blood & drowning in mud waves—I did not assist her, but tasted her blood & for an abominable second I desired— alas, I tremble writing such words—I longed to quench my thirst by drinking her. When licking the rubies from her neck, I discerned through the pouring rain the beating of her muscle of blood. Its pathetic echo joined the pernicious spasms of my own & then—I understood.

That same night I sewed her face, gave her the poppy wine, & held her hand to guide her through the pain. A young woman craving for what I despised the most— to be alive. In the nights that followed I lay on my bed nursing her body, warming her skin to absorb her febrile sweat. Every time I caressed her coal-black hair to calm her cries or opened the voluptuous curve of her pink lips with my fingers to pour the medicine in, my loins burned like sinners must burn in Hell.

She healed & I observed that, because of the colour of her skin, Mrs McTavish & the servants considered her a monstrous creature. Don't you find this the most interesting? Because they do respect me for my clear skin, although my soul is dark as a putrid tomb.

*I tried to hide myself from her in apathy & indifference, but two nights ago—oh dear, that night—she came to me—a dark **bean sìth**—& took me as no man should be taken. I was terrified of losing myself in her flesh, forgetting my humanity in the lustful yell of her body.*

*In case my poetics confuse you, I will confirm that yes, we did what in Medicine is known as coition—the precise introduction of the **membrum virile** inside the **feminine genitalia**. She opened her legs & guided me inside & for the first time I felt it, warm & wet, more delectable than* *any fondle, since it wrapped the delirium concentrated in that sole part of my body. (I should not tell you this, I know, I should not, I should not) She swung & caressed herself while I noticed how she grabbed me tighter with her guts to bring me deeper & further. Trepidation invaded my limbs as I thought something terrible might happen to me, because at the end of all that rapture I was sure there was darkness—dead darkness. So I repressed myself the best I could – even if that implied turning pleasure into acute pain. Yet I lost them—the strength, the reason, the fear. I was left empty as never before. No desire, no craving for blood but just her, her, her.*

I have not forgotten that I swore I would never kiss any other lips than yours, but last night I might have broken that oath. I used to believe—as you taught me— that carnal pleasure was revolting, but I shall admit I was tempted now & then. Like those rare days of my travels, sailing the oceans, when I found myself lying in the captain's bed, my head clouded with rum, yet not drunk enough to forget him kneeling before me…

I should not, I should not tell you all this—

But you cannot deny—dear cousin—that you were the one who awoke in me that impulse. The day I turned thirteen our family visited Calton Hill to drink tea & contemplate the grey city of Edinburgh sparkling under the precious sun of late Spring. Tired of the blandness of the scones & the conversation, I fell asleep behind some bushes. I woke up when you tickled my cheeks with a daffodil. Your loose hair shone like that flower—I had been playing with it before, stealing your hairpins—oh, how you yelled & tried to burn me with the boiling water from the teapot. With your face so close to mine I saw a dark red spot growing under your nose & then a drop fell in my lips—so I tasted it. Then I licked your blood with the tip of my tongue—what a delicious flavour, not as bitter as the medicine you used to give me. You seemed to like that, as you did not complain but dragged me closer. You placed your hand on my breeches & caressed me—how innocently I welcomed the pleasure. Nonetheless, when I attempted to kiss your lips—your thin pale lips—you pushed me away, repugnance souring in your face.

I did not understand then your rejection. Was it my miscarried kiss? My engorgement? That same night I stood in front of the large mirror in my room & introduced my hands under my nightgown—thinking about you, touching myself until I cried from pleasure and shame—while looking at the reflection of my distorted face. Mortification made me grab—with dirty, sticky hands—my father's antimony bottle & I drank it all in three gulps.

The servants found me next morning. I had been vomiting my guts until conscience left me, my last thought being that you would love me again if I purged myself from all the debris.

I could not eat in weeks—even swallowing water was a torment. My only companion was the clock in front of my bed, his mournful tick-tock echoing the stabbing pain in my stomach. You never came to visit.

To cure me you sent me to learn medicine with Dr Jenner & after your ultimate rejection I had to bury myself in the Highlands. I am nothing to you but a monster you find repulsive & I cannot bear the disgust in the eyes of the one I love. Yet I cannot blame you because all that you did was try to save me. However, I see now that we altered nature's sacred principles—is it really fair that hundreds of children suffer & die just to save one? Because of that my soul will be forever poisoned.

This morning I opened my eyes to see her lying by my side, her dark shoulder under my chin—sweet soil & dried flowers scent. I kissed the lovely form of her spine & she turned back to me, her smile brighter than the sun in winter. Her warm hands drew me closer & that time was as easy as singing a nursery rhyme from childhood. When my body moulded into hers there were neither shame nor pain, just cleanliness & beauty.

Forgive me,

Charles Bilsland, MD

P.S. Please, do not send me your bloodstained handkerchieves anymore.

Chapter 14

I carried the medicine-box into the study. The Mother sat behind the desk where the doctor and I had rolled. The Father stood beside her, a stocky hound of watery eyes. The Brown Twin sat on the big table pounding needles on the shaking feathers of a young crow. The bird cawed, begging for my help, but, *Hermano*, I couldn't move in front of the Mother. Papers, skulls and tools had regained their positions, but there were spaces on the shelves, the broken jars gone like rotten teeth from a mouth.

[The house is losing its fangs.]

The Mother's eyes were dusty. It had been a week since the Father and the *nieve*, buried the Yellow Twin in the mountains.

'My child— how dare you—?'

Her screams rushed like a waterfall down the stairs.

When the day broke, the Big Parlour glittered with tiny shards of whisky bottles spread across it like frost. The animal skins that the Father kept as trophies were grey ashes in the fireplace.

The yard was wounded with hundreds of holes dug, but the *nieve*'s radiance blinded the Mother, so she couldn't find the-Yellow Twin.

'It's hydr— hyd— '

Alcohol had already set fire to the Father's cheeks.

'Hydrophobia.'

The Mother spoke only to the doctor.

'Who else is infected?' she asked him.

'The cook.'

'But you... have the... cure.' the Father said.

'I've been investigating a vaccine against rabies, yes. Here...'

I went closer so the doctor could open the drawers of

the medicine chest to take out the bottles.

'My child—'

'I can save your child, Mr McTavish.'

The doctor placed the bottles, scarlet as wet blood, on the desk.

'So far, how many deaths have you prevented?' asked the Mother.

The doctor rolled his shirt sleeves up to show her his arms. The *rojo* in the wounds had turned brown—because my spell healed them.

'I tested the vaccine on myself. Mad dogs bit me but I'm not infected.'

'Yes, we hunted them and—'

'I need more tests.' the Mother said, ignoring the Father's words.

'I shall do more.'

'I don't mean your tests, doctor. Mine.' She crossed her arms and stared at me. 'Vaccinate the Cook.'

'At that stage of the illness, I—'

'Then, vaccinate the *dubh*. We'll take her to the barn and free the mad dogs you keep there to study her reaction after their bites.'

I wanted to throw away the chest and run. The Brown Twin smashed the crow's claws with one of the Mother's colourful rocks.

'No!' The doctor hit the desk with the palm of his hands, bending over the Mother.

'Heavens, I didn't expect so little confidence in your own vaccine.'

'I possess entire confidence in my vaccine, Mrs McTavish, I assure you, but I must not allow '

'Doctor…' The Father staggered towards him. 'I know you can cure my child…' The Father turned his head to the Mother. 'He comes from the city, he reads… books.' He belched. 'Test the vaccine on me,' he begged.

'Very well—but I shall be with you during the experiment.' The doctor glanced at me, calming my shivering like a ray of sunshine in a cold night.

'Science requires sacrifices,' the Mother said, then she stood up.

I was the first one. I sat on a chair beside the thin light of the window. The Mother tugged at my gown but the doctor stopped her.

'I'll do this.'

He untied the ribbons of my shift to strip my shoulders. Then he took *tortuga*, like a small turtle, from the medicine chest: earthy body and sharp, nose. *Tortuga* dived down the crimson bottle. The Mother's pen scratched the pages of her feathered creature. My stomach was a boiling pot, and I stroked my belly. She didn't know that the doctor blessed it. That is why he was now feeding me with his *sangre*, because I wouldn't have my red moons anymore. To shield this flesh-seed my body, as the Mother's, would swell and change until the day it bursted into a raging tide.

'Hold your breath,' he mumbled.

[The pain is a northern wave on burning sand. Lightning shoots through my veins and pushes out my breath. There is a sour taste under my tongue.]

He made me press on the wound with a cloth before he turned to the other shoulder. 'Twice?' the Mother asked.

'To assure success. Avoid it in infants, though.'

'I understand.'

She kept writing, holding the feathered creature against her enormous belly.

Tortuga bit me again. I was sure she didn't understand what the doctor was really doing.

'I'll protect you,' he mouthed while he nudged my hand.

The Mother, the Brown Twin, and the Housekeeper stayed on the second floor of the barn, where sacks of straw were stored like dead bodies. Below there were three dogs inside a cage with bars like the Mother's iron fingers. Black and Orange jumped against the fence until their furs reddened. Grey gnawed at the bars.

[The look in their eyes is the same as the Mainlanders who came and threw us away from our *Isla*. They grabbed *Madre* and *Padre* and tore...]

'She is to be naked.' The Mother pointed at me. For the dogs to bite her easily.'

'Naked?'

'You as well, doctor.'

'What?'

'Do as she says,' said the Father.

'But... Have you lost all—?'

'Do it.'

'Nonsense, I'll—'

The Father grabbed the doctor's waistcoat—both men wrestled—silver buttons flew in the air—the Father took a blow to the face—he swayed—bent—the doctor stopped—the Father hit the doctor's stomach with his head. The doctor fell on the floor, gasping like a fish pulled from the great sea

'Do it... or I'll... burst... your glass eyes.' The Father kicked him.

'*Dubh!*' The Mother's call, like knives caressing my skin, forced me to obey. Anger burnt my body, but soon my limbs felt cold when the clothes that protected them turned into a moult around my feet.

[The Mainlanders also tear my clothes before you save me and we run away—]

The doctor undressed and his sweat mixed with the stink of dung and rotten straw.

'Go and open the cage,' said the Mother to the

Housekeeper.

'Mistress, I beg you... dogs... they'll call the *bhampair*...'

The Mother hit the Housekeeper with the hissing cane until she cried tears and blood. The doctor's horse neighed. The Father grunted and opened the cage.

The doctor pushed me away and ran to the dogs.

The Brown Twin was looking at me. Ibiji. My *ojo* became a frozen ball. He knew where my other *ojo* was. Orange barked at the Father and then jumped on him. Frost imprisoned my limbs. Black, tail erect, was growling at the doctor. The Ibiji's stare was making the dogs become mad. Grey moved its head backwards and forwards, then lay on the floor, pawing the dirty straw. Dark flying worms.

[The Ibiji is possessing the dog.]

The revelation melted my paralysis and I ran to the horse, muscles tight at the promise of pain.

The dogs barked. I looked behind me. Orange and Black were on the doctor. Jaws gobbled down flesh. The doctor screeched and I screeched too. Grey dragged itself in my direction. I kicked the half door. Grey was closer, mouth foaming, lemon eyes turning to meaningless black. I shoved the door, the wood bit me. Neighs. The horse was Shangó, the God of War, and his hooves hit the door like battle drums. He would save me from the Ibiji and his evil games.

'*Obakosó kísi ekó sea akuni...*'

[The spasms of Grey's sick body claw the air around me.]

'*...bururu buburuku kiton...*'

[My fingers touch the metal handle.]

'*...awo Obá shokotó...*'

[I twist it until my hand bleeds.]

'*...kaguo kano sole Shangó.*'

[It opens.]

[Shangó jumps out, the door slams into me.]

Blind silence.

[Blood splashes on to my breasts and cheeks. Hoary fur and bones smash into the mud. Orange and Black defy Shangó, but he roars and gallops along the barn. The doctor rolls away, hands covering his head, but the Father is not quick enough so Shangó kicks him against the wall. The straw drinks the *rojo*. The barn's doors break in a storm of splinters and Shangó vanishes into the noiseless night. Black and Orange snarl as they tear into the Father, who bawls like a dying stag.]

A shot was fired from the second floor.

[I cough, casting out the dark smoke that poisons my lungs.]
    Orange was just a sack of smelly fur and black cries.
    The Father was silent.
    The doctor crawled towards him with the smile of his ribs moving up and down. He buried his head in the Father's chest and it seemed to me he was drinking his heart. I pulled the doctor's arm until his wild eyes—blue whirlpools in a red sea—looked at me. There were rubies hanging in his eyelids and his chin dripped.
    [He presses my hand, my bones scream.]
    He swung and lowered his head, I thought he was going to be sick but he coughed up blood instead and found his silver circles.
    '*Ve, ve...*'
    I pushed him towards the Mother, who was still holding fire-bird. The Brown Twin hummed behind her.
    Limping, the doctor climbed the stairs to the second floor.

Uno,
    dos,
        tres.
            [He falls]
                Cuatro,
                    cinco.
[Brown straw and *sangre* on his hands]

Seis,
siete.

[The Mother holds fire-bird tight]

Ocho,
nueve,
diez.

[Mouths scream all over his body, spitting *sangre*]

Once,
doce.

[His hair sparkles]

Trece.

[He is not the doctor but Obatala, claiming his own.]

[Black barks in a corner, calling Oshun, the Mother of the Dead.]

The doctor grabbed the fire bird and threw it away.

[Black mourns]

The Mother fell to her knees, holding the Brown Twin, staring at the animals.

[Black howls]

Chapter 15

20th March

Mo duine does not breathe. I barely feel his heartbeats. The doctor filled the wound in his chest with his cravats & sewed it. No hole can be noticed now.

The doctor says we should bury him.

21st March

The doctor buried *mo duine* in the yard. I have seen badgers digging far deeper dens.

Later. Cinnamon helped me carry the cook's body to the yard. When I was throwing mud at his face his eyes opened. This was surely a trick of the moonlight, as he last breathed in the morning.

~~The doctor must believe that *mo duine*'s body remains under the yew.~~

22nd March

The housekeeper thinks that the *bhampair* ate the cook. I tried to explain her that such a creature does not exist. The *Systema Naturae* provided some relief—I threw it at her to silence her whines.

29th March

The heavy rains from last week flooded the pantry & rotted the potatoes. The kitchen stinks like a ploughed

cemetery.
    Chewing oats bloats our abdomens.

~~*Later. Mo duine does not eat. If only I had meat for him.*~~

1st April

I collected oak galls, coperas & gum Arabech to make more ink. I discovered that the doctor had taken the sharpest crow quills to build his device to transfuse blood.
    I scratched his spectacles with the studio key when he was asleep.
    Blood Transfusion Apparatus:
    2 crow quills
    1 ureter (dog?)

Later. This apparatus reminded me of *Tractatus de Corde*. I completely disagree with its author, Dr ~~Lowre~~ Lower. This Englishman transfused animal blood into humans.

3rd April

I have taken the doctor's blood transfusion apparatus. ~~As I cannot feed *mo duine*, I trust that my blood will revitalise him.~~

Later. My petticoat has mildew. I cut it.

4th April

Yesterday I lay in bed when I heard a queer tune. It guided me to the Blue Room, where I saw the doctor leaning on the harpsichord, rocking oddly. When I discovered my *dubh* beneath him, I understood.

The doctor pulled back & she saw me. Rearranging her petticoat, she tried to run away. I held her, this not being an easy task, to reach between her legs where I felt ~~with delight~~ that the copulation had been consummated. I need further research but the doctor, stunned (to the point of being unable to button his breeches), stumbled over me & my *dubh* escaped.

7th April

Thousands of flies emerged from the oats & the crows stole the food we had left; their nests look like tumours infesting the bare branches in the yard.

I made the housekeeper eat the flies. A punishment for letting the crows devour our food.

Later. Blood from the ~~subclaw~~ subclavian artery is too thick. I will try the *arteria mameria externa*.

9th April

I woke up with Cinnamon gnawing at my forearm in dreams. To calm him, I gave him my breast, although I could not express milk from it.

The doctor suggested boiling the tablecloths, assuring me that cotton is quite nutritious. I wonder if he learnt this from his days in the South West of

England, where people (like sheep) enjoy eating grass.

Later. The dog's ureter I am using to transfuse blood is not long enough. I unburied the cook & used his, still in a reasonably good condition.

10th April

My *dubh* vomited into one of the kitchen pots. Despite the stench, my mouth produced an unusual secretion of saliva at the sight of the warm substance. Its colour reminded me of scrambled eggs.

The doctor examined her & concluded she ate poisonous berries.

I will perform an uroscopy on my *dubh*.

13th April

The housekeeper was quite agitated after discovering the black veins beneath the tablecloth on the Blue Room's desk. So much distress about my anatomical table, the display of dissected human veins, nerves & arteries on a varnished wooden surface.

~~*Later.* I found myself scratching the veins on the anatomical table. They tasted salty, like the weeds from the lake. The doctor saw me & — eventually — joined me.~~

~~Under the moonlight, the bloodstains left by our fingertips looked purple. My tongue burnt with wood splinters & his teeth were black. Yet the murmur of our mouths munching comforted me, scaring the~~

~~night away.~~

14th April

Recently, the doctor's favourite pastime is taking a stroll through the woods. He always comes back with an extravagant collection of plants, roots, fungi & colourful berries.

~~Later.~~ The uroscopy turned out to be a challenge. The bloodstains on my dress will be difficult to remove. I intended to cut my *dubh*'s bladder, but during the incision she broke the ropes that kept her at the operation table. I find her strength particularly surprising in this period of starvation. I calmed her screams; my wooden bookend came in quite handy. I solved the urine collection problem using a catheter, but sadly it has been left unsuitable for future tests.

According to the Urine Wheel, the tone, temperature & flavour denote pregnancy. Considering that it has been 9 days since the copulation, the gestation cycle in the Negro race appears short, as in the case of rats & other members of the *Mus* family.

15th April

The doctor entered my room & punched me. Then he knelt down beside me. I could not take my eyes off his raw knuckles. He caressed my face until his fingers turned red.

Later. Although he fixed my lips with needle & thread, my right cheek still feels numb.

16th April

The doctor offered me roots to eat. I refused them but accepted his leather medicine case. At least it has some animal substance.

I hid the candles because Cinnamon was eating them.

17th April

The doctor is to teach me how to use his blood transfusion apparatus properly. I was missing an important piece: the rubber plump.

Blood transfusion procedure
>Extracting blood from the donor:
>Tie a ribbon tightly on the upper arm to locate the *Median Basilic* Vein.
>Use a lancet to perform a 3 in. incision.
>Insert the quill.
>Let the blood drip into a recipient during 2 min, 12 oz.

Transfusing blood to the patient:
>Tie a ribbon tightly on the upper arm to locate the *Median Basilic* Vein.
>Use a lancet to perform a 3 in. incision.
>Insert the quill.
>Pour the blood into the conduit.
>Press the rubber plump.

18th April

The doctor drew my blood into a bowl. He drank it because it is very important to taste the temperature. Transfusing hot blood causes burns & ultimately death. Since my blood was too warm he repeated the procedure until I felt dizzy & lost conscience.

Later. ~~I spent 2 hours naked in the yard to cool my blood before transfusing it to mo duine.~~
   ~~I do not like the black hue on his chest.~~

~~23rd April~~ 25th April

Fever.
   This morning the doctor came to check my baby. ~~When I had him between my thighs, his ear pressed to my belly, I felt the ardour of a revelation. He is the only man & I am the only woman.~~

~~26th April~~

~~The housekeeper claims that the *bhampair* is drinking me. Nonse~~

27th April

The doctor feeds me some sour, blue blend. He says our children are well, but I cannot have them close because of the fever.

Later. There was grass growing through the wooden boards of my bedchamber. I had to get up to uproot it with the doctor's scalpel. He watched me from the bed & laughed.

29th April

My *dubh* stabbed the doctor's hand with a carving knife. Then she ran out of the house after him, screaming. So far, neither of them is back.

Later. I am inclined to believe that negresses might have the impulse to cannibalise the male after mating.
 Notes on my dubh's *pregnancy.*
 Morning nausea.
 Increase of her aggressive behaviour.

30th April

Cinnamon hunted a horse in the woods. I helped him dismember the animal & we carried the pieces home.

Later. The doctor is back. Nothing he says makes sense, meat, blood & mad cats.

2nd ~~March~~ May

Cinnamon has been bitten in the most savage way. I will slaughter the animal that did this.

 Cinnamon's injuries
 2 in. cut in the forearm.

~~*Later.* The housekeeper blames the *bhampair*. She insists that the monster is hiding into the old well & even suggested I should go there to see it myself. I cannot stand her anymore.~~

~~Bhampair?~~
~~Fore teeth — Conic, 6 in each jaw?~~
~~Tusks — Long.~~
~~Grinders — With conic projections?~~
~~Food — Preying on human blood.~~

4th May

The ~~housek~~ horse meat was too dry. I hope Cinnamon will recover his colour soon.

Later. Who harmed my child? The doctor & my *dubh* are the only ones left.

6th May

The *bhampair* is none other than my *dubh*. Noctambulism, aggressiveness, small size & dark colour match the habits & appearance of the creature.

I will open her uterus to extract the foetus, the most fascinating case of study in my research! I should ask the doctor for assistance. I fear that his right hand (still bandaged) might have lost its ability in surgery.

7th May

I woke up with my shift wet around the thighs. There was some bloo

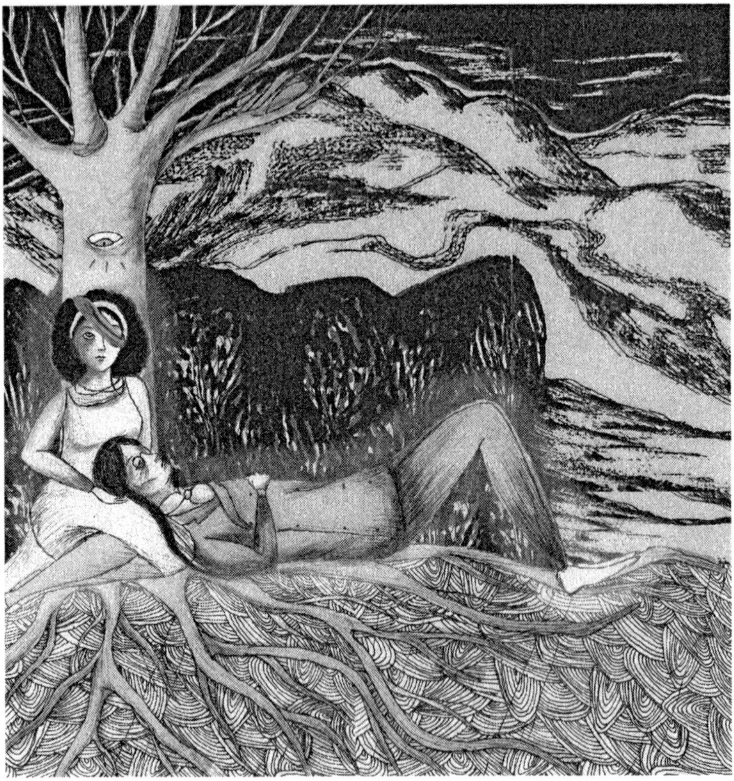

Chapter 16

A rattle woke me. Through the curtain of my hair I saw the doctor pissing into the chamber pot beside the bed. These days our stomachs were like abandoned dens. Bones grew sharp, skin turned hard, and winter blew in our lungs.

The mattress shook. I buried my face into the curve of his neck. His hair made my skin itchy.

'I dreamed of you,' I said.

He embraced me tighter.

'We were in the house, but...' Words came out of my mouth like water from a mountain spring. 'They wanted us, but you took me to this hole, *madriguera*, and we run it... there's *luz*... and the sky is *gris*, and the ground, and there are high buildings, and the people, and the metal monsters, roughing, smoke, but you say— you—'

'Don't cry...'

He pulled my hair back.

'Say you cannot be a doctor there, nevermore. We climb this hill and there is a big wave is... very big...'

'It's just a—'

'The wave... *zash*, and you hold me but I don't know... if I can find you nevermore under the wave...'

'Shh...' He kissed my tears. 'Shh...'

In the Mother's bedchamber the air was dying. The doctor used the frozen metal snake that he called 'sick-siphon' to seal the Mother's marbled lips so the *abiku* couldn't escape from her. [It will get hungry soon and start devouring the Mother's entrails.] After she had attempted to uproot my own baby, the White God sewed my torn skin with a magic spell and calmed my guts with rose water. Now the Mother lay on the bed burning in the the *abiku*'s gluttony-fire. I was so hungry, sour blueberries were not enough.

Curtains, tablecloths, chairs... I wanted to eat the whole house. Under my dress, my nipples hurt. The doctor's hands, quick as birds, confined the sick-siphon in a red velvet cage.

[I want him.]

He bent over to listen to the Mother's heartbeats. I remembered him bending over me every night, his flesh melting and his voice breaking when he called me *'ma mystique prune...'*

'She's getting worse.' The doctor clasped the Mother's hand to finish his incantation.

'Her blood is boiling.'

I took the doctor's metallic claw and started ripping the buttons from the Mother's dress. I grabbed one of her breasts. It felt soft and heavy. I went over the circle of her nipple with the claw's blade. *Rojo* slid down the sheets. The Mother's eyelids trembled, like ripples on water.

The doctor pushed me away, removing the blade ('scalpel' he calls it, it sounds like a demon's name) from my hands. The *oscuridad* in his eyes yelled at me.

[*Hermano*, I don't recognise him now.]

'Take her, she is ready.'

He shook his head and stepped back, pushing the candlestick off the three-legged table. I hurried to step on the flame that had been born on the carpet. I tasted smoke on the tip of my tongue. When I looked up, the doctor was already gone.

I found him in the kitchen. The copper pots stared at us, filled with dust and grime. The air reeked of potato-dead. I had poisoned them with piss and shit I took from the chamber pots. The potatoes were innocent, but I had to do it to weaken the Mother. I had also nursed pearly maggot eggs in the dried food, praying for the insects to break out ravenous.

The doctor grasped a carving knife.

'I won't—do—it again,' he gasped. 'I won't do it. I am not— I am no— doctor anym—'

The oak table roared when he stabbed his right hand with the carving knife, and he groaned and bent down, like a tree in a storm.

I saw the Mother tottering across the door, her loose hair like a dried bush. Her dress was unbuttoned, showing her flushed breast collapsed onto her belly. She started scratching a spell on her feathered creature. She wanted her revenge.

[I must remove the knife before the incantation is finished.]

'*Obatala dibeniwua binike ala lo laa...*'

I pulled the handle. The doctor ran away, leaving a red ghost on the table.

Outside, everything was thick blue. Clouds hung over my head like sea foam. The mountains darkened my way downhill, but blood was the lantern that guided me throughout the white grass. My feet drowned in putrid mushrooms, carrion-feed, and dead leaves: the spring's afterbirth.

'Doctor...'

Blackthorn-claws made my arms cry *rojo*.

'I can't—'

He was at the riverside, holding his hand as if it was an injured animal.

'Doctor...'

'I can't— the ginger girl, she— the nun gave me the bowl full of blood and— oh God, I drank her— I—' He waved in the direction of the house. 'I'll drink them all, they're dead, they're— the vaccine doesn't work, they'll die, like the ginger girl, I drank her and all the children from the Under City— I can't do this anymore—'

'Doctor...'

'I'm no doctor, there's no doctor, there never was— I'm a monster— can't you just—?' He snatched my shoulder and shook me. *Lluvia*, the pouring rain, beat the river. 'I drank everyone who came to me seeking comfort. I fed on their diseases, I sucked their fluids from the operation table and licked the tools I used to open them, and Miss Bilsland, and Mrs McTavish, oh, I drank them as well, and I drank you, because I didn't want to die—'

He forced me to face the coming-river, and the river laughed, and then I understood he wanted to feed me to the river. I fought him back, swinging the carving knife and biting the air.

'I can't— can't—' he kept repeating.

Lluvia numbed my limbs and filled my eye. Water washed away his wrinkles. His mouth opened, diamonds sparkling on the silver circles around eyes. I followed his line of sight.

Shangó was in front of us, white mane flowing into the air. *Espíritus* rode the rain, gathering in the form of silver clouds around his muzzle. His legs, thin like young poplars' trunks, seemed to have rooted in the ground. I untied myself from the doctor's embrace and went to Shangó. The air smelled of new-born pines.

I caressed his mane.

'*Gracias.*'

Lluvia was drawing changing pictures on Shangó's skin. I lost myself in the constellations reflected in his almond eyes. My *ojo*? Can Shangó see where they kept my *ojo*? I held my breath to keep my soul pure.

I cut the horse's throat.

Sangre poured down all over me like mystic rain. Shangó wailed and crumpled to the ground, offering himself to the White God. The trees convulsed, and their leaves bursted into thousands of flying ravens. The doctor

fell to his knees, hands covering his face. He was crying.
I threw the knife away and rushed to him.
'For you, Shangó give you his blood, see?'
The doctor yelled.
'*Tienes que beber su sangre. Bébela.* Understand?'
[I strip his hands off his face.]
'Drink his *sangre* to grow strong, drink Shangó…'
[I lick his grief: water, blood, mud and mucus.]
'Drink, *bébela*, drink, drink.'

Light-splash flies danced around Shangó's head. *Lluvia* had dried, like the doctor's wails.

>'*En la mar hay una torre,*
>*En la torre una ventana,*
>*En la ventana hay una hija*
>*Que a los marineros ama.*
>
>*Las estrellas del cielo*
>*Una y una se hacen dos.*
>
>*Dame tu mano paloma*
>*Para subir a tu nido.*
>*Maldicha que duermes sola*
>*Vengo a dormir contigo.*
>
>*Si la mar era de leche,*
>*Los barquitos de canela,*
>*Pescaría las mis dolores*
>*Con palabrillas de amor.*
>
>*Las estrellas del cielo*
>*Una y una se hacen dos.*
>
>*Dame tu mano paloma*

Para subir a tu nido.
Maldicha que duermes sola
Vengo a dormir contigo.'

I sang *Madre*'s lullaby. *Blanco* sun shed light on the dandelions, Oshun's eyes watching over me. I've been her spirit-daughter since the day I was born in the Isla and *Padre* held me to her. The grass had turned orange. Sparkling trees freed their arms from the ivy's embrace and extended to scrape the sky. Gold, dry-blood, purple. The clouds were on fire.

The doctor rested his head on my lap. Our arms were tangled together while he drew red stripes on my belly.

'*Je vais vous donner mon sang'.*

The smell of melting copper and rotten fish made me feel sick. I belched.

[Behind the bushes, the Brown Twin is staring at us.]

Chapter 17

Glēfian, Wed. 2nd May

Dear Dr Jenner,

I truly, ~~truly, truly~~ appreciate the delicacy of your sile-ce.

~~Ahh~~ Words might be scalpels, but the abs--ce of them is ana e s t h e tic, as the applicati~ of snow on a blue bruise. ~~Snow~~ W~ter froze our fri--dship, but tis for the sake of that summer that I write – also, yours is the oly address I ca~ remember.

I beg your pard~ for my terrible h a n d w r i t i n g. I'm forc-d to use my left h~d – but the worst thīg is the smell of the right oē, like the Norl Loch ~ Ed~burgh or a~ August day.

H y d r o p h o b i a murtherud 6 5 in the mansio~. Just 3 – Mrs McT, the Girl & me – rema~

if not safe, at least free from the distemper's bite.

Never the less, as black pineS fīd ī corpses the alimēt to e~hance their awful greeess,

I've also gather'd know ~valuable know l e d g e about this slaughter.

H y d r o p h o b i a isnt o-ly tra~smitt'd by the bite of mad animalS, but also by the digestiom of ~fect'd blood. The McT ate nfect'd dogS & squirrelS' raw meat—I discover'd this too late. Mr McT h---d them to feed the

113

family in w--~ter.

It progresses at a different pace depend~g on the pati--. O-~ McT twin was bitten by a rabid kitten i^ October, but just in February the ve~o~ on his blood xt~guish'd him. This demōstrates that ōly I—who already surviv'd it—& the Girl—she was never allow'd to eat meat & I also vaccīat'd her—are truly safe from the disease.

Mrs McT also ate raw meat. Therefore, it may spurt at any hour, a~y day. She is pregn pregnat—~close to her due date. I dread the moment whe~ I have to assist her ī the delivery, as my right ha~d is useless & I'm suffer~g from dizzii~ess episodS.

For those who are already ill, the vaccinat~~ isn't effective. Thus, I've beeen performing a~ alternative treatment, the tr—sfus--- of my own blood——which possesses the memory of surviv--g it. I add it to the food & the water – I don't xtract more than 1/2 pt per day, as I've calculat'd they'd need at least 2 weekS to heal & I can~not be coNsum-d before that. The McT Twin is the most critical case – I'm trāsfusing blood to his mediā veī usīg a proper artificial device, please check the draw~~~gS I se~nd you.

His body is creamy & warm like a 1/2 bak'd biscuit, & to calm him I sing
There were 3 ravens sat on a tree They were
as black as they
~~could~~ might
be

& his cheekS are pī-k as a hedgehogs

D'you remember those hedgehogS you us-d to replicate Dr H's xperim--ts? It took you moths to realise that twas I who stole them from your studio to free 'em & yet you didn't beat me but told me
'COMPASSION IS WHAT MAKE S A GREAT DOCTOR'

I was only 13, but from that moment I wish'd to be that great dr myself, like you,

Dr Hunter
Dr Dyer
Dr Lower

<u>*Compassion*</u> *led me to assist your wife that unfortuuate night her Consumptio- got worse. Durong the day she'd suffer'd from severe coughi-g & bleedi-g. With you away in Lonnodonn – r--co—ter--g your fellow Freemaso-s – who do you thik they call-d?*

When I came Mrs J's breath was so— --the wīdow of her white lips clos-d with purple clots—that I thought you'd not 've time to bid her farewell. Instead of cuppin-g Mrs J, I decid-d to perform xperimental tr—t-ent & twas what you witness-d whē you appeard so u n e x p e c t e d l y.

The 3 wome- that lay on the floor were prostitutS— I'll not hide this detail—but their nudity & fat were-t product of carnal affair—but of the 3 pt of blood I xtract-d from them. If 1 was just a child, that's the

115

procurer's fault. C---der--g my devoirs as a dr, I only checkd her female apparatus to make sure she was free from veemereal diseasS.

The blood on the floor, the chairS, the curtainS & my own clothS belonged mai ~ly to the younug prostitute. Like her companionS, I also offer.d her a bottle of whisky mix'd with laudamum—20 gtt—to make her more receptive to the treatment—but she got intoxicat-d & vomitad all over me—that's why you fonnd me 1/2 naked. Whē I ope~d her legS to access her femoral artery, she got scared of the scarificator & kickeed out at my face & I—by mistake—sectioned quite a number of vesselS. The youmg prostitute started running aroūd the apartm.~t—& the more she rush'd, the more the wou~d opened. I was afraid that her screams would brīg the servanntS—they were already knocking on ~ the door— so I caught her & press-d her throat ūtil the absence of air & then you
  emtered & saw me sucki~g blood out of Mrs J's bosom.

  This wasnt an act of depravity but desperatio ~ ~.

I needd to xtract the poisonooous blood before injecting the vigorous one, but I fear'd that my tramsfusion e-q---still rudimentary back the~—would harm Mrs J's delicate vesselS. Not having much time to thik—& havinng drun~k the rest of the bottle o n my own—I decided to use my own mouth.

116

I swear to you & to God & God that I askad Mrs J's for permissio~ before u-butto--g her shift. Her lips failed in the pr---ciatio~ of recognisable wordS, but on her eyeS I read her yearn--g for life,

the yearn-~g of 1 who knows she's lov'-d & need-~'d in this world.

Mrs J recover'd – so I heard.

I u-dersta~d it now. God wa~ts me to give <u>my own blood.</u> He wants me to give

every

si~gle

drop

uutil my veins 're dri-d & my body cleonsed of SIN & degradatio~. Blood is my curse, but if I ca~ turn it o~to the m---cle that wiill allow otherS to live,

I shall die happy.
Pleas please please please plese plese plese plase please plese pleas plese plese please plege pleas plse pleak plse plede plege plee ple plase pleas plse pleas plase pleas plese pl pleas plase pleae plege please please pleas pleas pleas plse pleae plse pleae pleae plee ple plase pleas pleas plse pleae plse pleae pleae plee ple plase pleas plse plete pleae pleas plse pleae plse pleae pleae plge ple plase pleas plse pleae plase pleas plese plese plese plese plase plede plese pleas plese plese please pleae pleas plse plede plse pleae pleae plee ple plase pleas pls pleas plse pleae plse pleae pleae

plee ple plase pleas plse pleae plase pleas plese
pl pleas plase pleae pleas plse pleae plse pleae
pleae plse ple plase pleas plse pleae plase pleas
plese pl pleas plase plase pleas plse pleae plase
pleas plese plese plese plese plase pleae plese ple
plase pleas plse pleae plase pleas plese pl pleas
plase pleae pleas plse pleae plse pleae pleae pleae
please plede pleds pleas plse pleae plse pleae pleae
plee ple plase pleae pleas plse pleae plse pleae
pleae plee ple plase pleas plse pleae pleae pleas
plse pleae plse pleae pleae plee ple plase pleas plse
pleae plase pleas plese plse plese plese plase pleae
plese pleas plse plese plase plede pleas plse pleae
plse pleae pleae plee ple plase pleas pls pleas plse
pleae plse plede pleae plee ple plase pleas plse
pleae plase pleae pleas plse pleae plse pleae pleae
plee ple plase pleas pls pleas plse pleae plse pleae
pleae plee ple plase pleas plse pleae plase pleas
plese pl pleas plase pleae pleas plse plede plse
pleae pleae plse ple plase pleas plse pleae plase
pleas plese pl plase pleas plse pleae plase pleas
plese plese plese plese plase plede plese pleas plese
plese please pleae pleas plse pleae plse pleae pleae
plee ple plase pleas pls pleas plse pleae plse pleae
pleae plee ple plase pleas plse pleae plase pleas
plese pl pleas plase pleae pleas plse plede plse
pleae pleae plse ple plase pleas plse pleae plase
pleas plese pl pleas plase plase pleas plse pleae
plase pleas plese plese plese plese plase pleae plese
ple plase pleas plse pleae plase pleas plese pl pleas

plase pleae pleas plse pleae plse pleae pleae please
please pleae pleds pleas plse pleae plse pleae pleae
pleg ple please pleae pleas plse pleae plse pleae
pleae ple pl plese pl plase pleas plse pleae plase
pleas plse plese plese plese plase pleae plese pleas
plese plese please pleae pleas plse pleae plse pleae
pleae pleg ple plase pleas pls pleas plse pleae plse
pleae pleae plee ple plase pleas plse pleae plase
pleas plese pl pleas plase pleae pleas plse pleae
plse pleae pleae pleg ple plase pleas plse pleae
plase pleas plese pl pleae plase plase pleas plse
pleae plase pleas plese plese plse plese plase pleae
plese ple plase pleas lase pleas plese plese plese
plese plase pleae plese pleas plese plese please pleae
pleas plse pleae plse pleae pleae pleg ple plase
pleas pls pleas plse pleae plse pleae pleae plse ple
plase pleas plse pleae plase pleas plese pl pleas
plase p pleae plee ple plase pleas pls pleas plse
pleae plse pleae pleae plse ple plase pleas plse
pleae plase pleas plese pl pleas plase pleae pleas
plse pleae plse pleae pleae plse ple plase pleas plse
pleae plase pleas plese pl pleas pluse

Chapter 18

[I walk through the undulating grass. Black-headed gulls cut the sky. The sun illuminates spores— or is it *nieve*?— in the air. I climb the *montaña*, its breath on my face. *Viento* pulls silver new-born leaves off their branches. Cries. I hold it against my breast. *Abiku*.]

The Mother picked up the clock from the tea table and threw it in my direction, and it shattered against the wall.
'Damn!'
The doctor pushed me aside.
'*Dubh*.'
The Mother tried to grab my arm, but I stepped backward.
'*Dubh*.'
Her dress was a withered flower because the *abiku* had already swallowed her baby and grew inside her bloating belly and ankles, breast and fingers.
'*Dubh, dubh*...' the doctor mocked her.
'I need her, it's the last test before...' The Mother's face turned *rojo*. 'She's the *bhampair*, don't you see? She's...'. the Mother said, taking a chair leg from the floor. 'She drank the blood... *mo duine*... my children...'
[I stay next to the doctor. Her words don't frighten me anymore.]
'I explained to you yesterday, were you not listening?' she continued.
'Stop it.'
'*Dubh*.'
'Don't touch her.'
The doctor snatched the chair leg and threw it away.
'She's the *bhampair*... She'll kill us and the childr–'
'*Arrêtez-vous!*'

The doctor pushed her away.

Her hands clambered up his waistcoat like cockroaches, grabbing his cravat. The doctor coughed, then managed to seize her wrists. She pulled and bit his hair. Both fell to the ground. The Mother scratched his face and spat on his silver circles. The doctor struck her.

I knelt beside them, breathing in the Mother's pain while he hit her.

'My chi—' she whined. The doctor's body over hers was a white tide of screaming waves devouring the red shore.

Blanco y rojo.

'My chil—'

The doctor only stopped when he realised that most of the blood came from between her legs.

The Mother lay on her bed, tearing the sheets and foaming at the mouth. The doctor had cut her dress, and the tartan rags were drenched in coppery lumps. Her legs were open and her belly was boiling, but only a brown liquid smelling of vinegar came out.

'Breathe now...' The doctor let her clutch his healthy hand. 'Yes... there...'

The web of veins on her belly had turned purple. She groaned like a wounded boar. The doctor took a piece of wood and forced the Mother to bite it.

'Push...'

She clenched her teeth until her eyes rolled back, *blanco.*

'Hold, hold, hold there...' He slid his hand into her *coño*, seeking the *abiku*.

She retched.

'Water!' the doctor shouted at me while he held the Mother's neck to the side, orange-earth vomit running through his fingers.

Sweat streamed across down the Mother's face. Her blonde hair looked white in the midday sun entering through the window, while the veins on her belly had turned black, like cracks in a snowed *montaña*. There were dried faeces between her thigh, and the reek of dead flesh mixed with the scents of rancid wine and wet dog fur. I cleaned her with a soaked cloth, my stomach shivering with terror-cold.

The doctor stroked water over her face.

'Mrs McTavish…'

Her eyes were thin blue lines between the dark eyelids.

'Open…'

She mumbled.

'Mrs McTavish…' He felt her forehead. 'You're burning.'

The doctor caressed her cheek.

'Open…'

'I can't, my—'

He lifted his bandaged hand.

'Open…'

The Mother turned her head to the wall.

I went to the lame table where his glittering tools lay in a pile and took the sharpest one. The *abiku* had eaten too much. Because of its quick growth it was trapped inside the Mother's belly, with no space even to open its jaw. I could imagine its sticky skin, not white any more but coloured with blood and bile, and its body, a fleshy bag full of regurgitated meat and hairs, dripping corroding saliva. Now that the *abiku* was probably too lazy to even burp the doctor had to take it out.

'Open,' I repeated, offering him the metallic claw.

He covered his face and started shaking.

Sangre.

Under the green light of dawn, the Mother looked at me, eyes full of red clouds. All her screams had escaped through the open window, leaving her empty. Her fingers rubbed my hand and I held them.

The Mother's belly had cracked: *océanos* of *rojo* and yellow thick foam in which organs sank like stranded ships. All her secrets exposed, like the pictures in the feathered creatures she stared at before torturing me.

[I caress the maroon worms that spill from her belly on to the bed.]

[*Hermano*, remember that maroon sunrise when we arrived to Leith's port?
My fingers leave a red track on the white lace sheets.]

> '*Soltadla… no la toquéis…*'
> > You cried when they caught me.
> 'I don't need white.'
> > The Mother said, so her men beat you.
> > > And beat you.
> > > And beat you.

[I pull the worm out, looking for myself in her eyes.]
> > > And beat you.
> You were drowned in red and I was strangled with the
> > > > Mother's words.
> > 'Black is fascinating.'
> > > She killed you.

[I wrap the Mother's worm around my neck.]

Ahora todo lo tuyo es mío.

There was a scent of copper and old lemons when I squeezed the Mother's liver. It felt like drenched moss. The doctor had pulled the *abiku* out her pink pocket of flesh. Only pieces of the dried cocoon were left inside. I heard wood cracking and I thought it was the house collapsing at last. Then I realised the noise was born in the Mother's guts and travelled through her throat to come out from her blue lips.

'Mère...'

The doctor was curled up beside the bed.

'Mère, mère...'

He clenched the sheets.

'Mère...'

'Obatala eruye aye aye mogua ye...'

I knelt in front of the White God.

'Gracias.'

My curse had been successful.

'Mère aidez moi...'

He buried his face in the sheets, feeding that cottony *nieve* with *sangre* and sweat. I took the mewling bundle from his lap before leaving.

When I reached the top of the *montaña*, dark clouds chased the *abiku* in my arms. I placed the creature on a rock blessed by late *nieve*. Its purpose had been accomplished and it must return to the *Blanco*. I was setting sixteen white pieces of broken cups around it when I heard steps. I turned back to meet a couple of watery eyes framed by cinnamon curls. His rags stank of excrements and grease— [the Brown Twin is staring at the *abiku*.] He understood.

The boy took something from under his shirt. A little jar. Hail. It started hailing. The *abiku* cried, the glass surface sang.

The Brown Twin gave it to me. It wass filled with golden water, and inside, floating...

My *ojo*.

My *ojo*, alone, dull, blind without the reflection of my precious memories.

My black *ojo*.

He was offering me my *ojo* hoping I would ask the *abiku* not to devour him in return.

[I grab the jar.]

My...

Out.

Chasing me.

Rain.

Lluvia.

The beast.

I ran.

Burning saliva and mad eyes.

He opened.

I cried.

Bare trees puncturing my skin.

Claws.

An icy bite.

Dientes.

Teeth.

[Yellow thunders in my brain.]

[I breathe mud.]

Lluvia.

Rain.

Sangre.

He was the one.

[I yell, and fire consumes my guts and turns my throat into ashes.]

[Clouds groaned, mountains howl, black pines shriek and gulls whine. All of them acknowledge my grief, all except *el sordo*, the one who can't hear, who can't perceive. His face, where hunger dug holes, remains unchanged. I can't stand it.]

[He must feel.]

[I throw the jar at his head, and my fury turns the glass into fangs that devour his features and dissolve them in red saliva. I push him and he falls backwards and rolls downhill until his body is nothing but a chunk of meat in the *montaña*'s jaws.]

[I laugh,
and scream,
and cry,
and yell.]
[The *abiku* keeps mewling.]

[I still can hear the cries when I curl inside the trunk of a dead oak. My body is numb when I feel a small fish splashing inside my belly. My heart jumps, awaiting another manifestation, but I don't sense it anymore, it's gone. The cadaverous face of the house is the last thing I see.]

[¹Hooves are battering the ground…]

---

[1] And from here, Mrs Luna went silent and refused to tell me anything else.

Chapter 19

Duncansburgh, 1st June 1804

Dear Miss Bilsland,

My heart sickens more with each word I write. Dutifully following the request in your letter, I travelled to the West Highlands to meet your cousin, my former apprentice & dear friend. Amongst the sharp rocks of Glenfinnan I reached the McTavish mansion, but the family was gone; evidence suggests they might have left in distress & perhaps violence. At Duncansburgh, the soldiers assumed this to be the result of an old dispute between Scotch clans, widely known for their cruelty & depravity. Nevertheless, God would not permit me to discover a single hint of your cousin's whereabouts, might he be alive or—I beg the Almighty not to allow this—victim of some terrible attack.

My prayers & most compassionate thoughts are with the Bilsland family, such gentle friends & supporters of my research, in this moment of darkness & grief.

Your very humble servant & affectionate friend,

Edward Jenner MD

28th April

Hives

Travellin' from Glasgow to the Highlands. Leavin' the city in clarity, I ventur'd out into this oneiric land of shadows & uncertainty. Trees like an old woman's hand shakin' in her last hour. Houses like graves. Smal lights glitterin' in the distance like fairy fires. The day might be beyond the mist.

2 May

Hives
Costiveness

The coach agravated my distress. Had to stop at midday.
Slow fever? Tartar emetic to purge. Need to ask the innkeeper for roten fruit. If not, constipation can be cur'd with **mercurus chloride** *infusion?*
The red bumps on my forearm could be the first warnnin' signs of Measle. A hot bath is requir'd with the most urgency.

Later. *Pain didn't allow me to sleep. Smokin' popies made me remember. The Bilsland boy & me at Dr Hunter's studio. Dr H had bought Mr Bilsland's stilborn daughter—God! is there anything that Jacobite wouldn't have exchanged for laudanum's liquor? Had just start'd cuttin' when Dr H push'd me aside sayin' my fingers were like 'fat maggots'. He turn'd to praise the Bilsland boy's 'little fingers, nimble as albino grasshoppers'. The B boy was 10? 11? 'This is your half-sister, so be gentle,'*

Dr H advis'd the child before givin' him the brain knife.

That night the B boy crept to my bed. 'Did I kill her?' I said she never liv'd. How he cri'd, the dark midget. 'Let's put all the pieces back tomorrow,' he made me prommise.

6 May

Costiveness
Dyspepsia

Duncansburgh. Soldiers, peasants, a few prostitutes. A Mr Puttock explain'd me the McTavish haven't been seen around yet, their mansion is left isolat'd durin' the winter & there's still white on the mountains. Mr Puttock will be my guide & 2 soldiers will come to aid us with the snow, the Bilsland money help'd to convince them all.

Later. Pain around my navel. Cramp colic?

7 May

Asthenia
Biliousness
Costiveness

Set camp in the midle of the forest. Felt so sick I couldn't even ride the horse. Must be food poisonin' – that venison sauc'd with cinammon & cloves that I ate at Duncansburgh.

8 May

The mansion was like a black monster lyin' on the snow. The mansion. Enter'd. A large parlour. Mr Puttock & the soldiers started checkin' the rooms, callin' out for the McTavish. Notic'd some screws & gears on the floor. A smash'd clock. Stench of wet dog & rotten wood. Discover'd a brown stain on the floor. Couldn't move a limb. Brown stain shap'd like a liver. Heard the soldiers screammin' upstairs. Remember'd cries, howls & mad cows, I'm a child of 6 tryin' to survive Small Pox in blackness. Realis'd my fingers were turnin' numb. Realis'd I was steppin' on the snow in the yard.

    Couldn't go back.

10 May

> ***Biliousness***
> ***Synochus***
> ***Asthenia***
> ***Dyspepsia***
> ***Costiveness***

The B boy is in a cell, still lethargic. Scars & incisions all over his body. Keep him warm. Duncansburgh's people want the neygress dead. They believe her to be the perpetrator of the slaughter. Convinc'd the soldiers to let me see her—more Bilsland money! Her upper lip was broken & her cheeks swolen with haematomas. She couldn't speak, just sobbed. Detect'd a slightly bloatt'd belly—pregnancy? Half of her face is scarr'd & her left eye is gone; an old injury. How could this pathetik creature have been capable of such horror?

11 May

Asthenia
Synochus
Dyspepsia

The B boy is awake. He doesn't speak. Doubt he recognises me – I'm reliev'd. Fed him soup & soggy bread.

They want to burn the neggress. Paid more, sayin' I haven't conclud'd my examination of her.

Later. Remember'd December 1794, when putrid fever almost kill'd me. No one dar'd to approach that bed where I boil'd in my own fluids. Making peace with God when my febrille eyes glimpsed a white apparition: the B boy. He open'd all the windows in the apartment. Fresh, violent air. He undres'd me & clean'd my body with a linen cloth. His white fingers inside my ears, on my hipbones, below my knees, between my toes. Felt like a cloud blessin' my limbs.

12 May

Asthenia
Tympany
Dyspepsia

The B boy refuses to speak English. Brought some of my garments to dress him properly. He had to tie the breches with a rope. 3 soldiers & 1 magistrate from Glasgow *brought the neggress to the cell. She start'd screamin' as soon as she saw him. 1 of the soldiers slapp'd the neggress' face & I caught the unfortunate in my arms before she faint'd. Ask'd her with sweet words what caused her more distress. She cri'd a torrent of words, in different languages, but I caught '**bhampair**', 'dr' & 'baby.' My heart jump'd to my mouth when I understood what she was tryin' to tell us. The B boy devoured the baby. Said so aloud & the B boy became insane. The 3 soldiers had to detain the beast – howlin' some French gibberish.*

Bowels drown in sorrow.

Must speak to the magistrate.

13 May

Tympany
Cynanche maligna
Synochus

I confess'd the truth about the B boy. Couldn't hide my tears of shame, for indeed I am partially responsible for the McTavish' deaths.

Later. Does Miss Bilsland know? Dr Hunter told me she gave the B boy a special tonic when he was a child to cure his physical weakness. This revitalissing tonic was made of children blood. How can the Scotch say they fear God & then perpetuate such barbarism?

Violence must run in the Scotch blood. These mountains are like fangs, these valleys like starving guts.

14 May

Epistaxis
Melancholia
Cynanche maligna

Duncansburgh's too distress'd to wait for a trial. The McTavish were a sort of native chiefs around here & the Scotch want revenge. Fearin' for another Jacobite rising, I felt extremmely reliev'd when the magistrate call'd for an emergency execution first thing next mornin'.

The B boy has high temperature. Wash'd his face with fresh water & made him drink popy juice. His right hand is in an advanc'd state of mortification.

Later. He made me understand he wanted a 'last favour.' Couldn't see why he need'd his hand amputat'd since soon he'd not need any limb of his body & the prospect of touchin' him was repulssive. Seeing his fake tears didn't move me, he grabb'd my cravat & yell'd & burden'd with his malignity, I had to consent. Brought a lanthorn & put the apron on. Sharpen'd the muscle knife & the saw before adjustin' the screw-tourniquet to his wrist. Fear froze my lungs to the point of asphyxiation – or was it because of the foul smell? His hand was white no more, fingers turn'd into chunks of black flesh with green nails dripin' a brownish juice. Through his scratch'd glasses I glimpsed the mad stare behind his dark eyes – God, how could I have confus'd depravity with pure devilisshness? His sweaty face crumpl'd & grey skin peel'd off it, revealin' somethin' that couldn't be human.

The 1st cut wasn't quite clean 'cause of my arm's

lack of strength. In the 2nd I shiver'd whilst containin' nausea. After the 3rd he snatch'd the knife & did it himself. Tendons burst. His face turned green & then white. Tack'd the arteries away with needles. Souless groans when I was shatterin' the bone. Took his hand apart & felt sick – it had the stench of decomposin' corpses drownin' in a faecal pond. Buri'd his veins in tissue skin & sutur'd. Retch'd on the table but don't think he mind'd, by that time he'd already faint'd. Bandag'd the stump. Left the room.

15 May

In the coach to Glasgow. Couldn't stay in that cursed place a minute more. The Bilslands? A letter will do. Got the B boy's medical diaries in my suitcase. Couldn't keep myself from takin' them when nobody was lookin'. Will donate them to the University of Edinburgh. After that I'll forget – forget even Scotland exists.

Black smoke rose from the gaol whilst I heard an enrag'd crowd pourin' into the buildin'. Wonder if it was 'cause I let the neggress escape. God knows she's innocent, but I hope she's also smart enough to put to good use the horse & the money I gave her.

NOW EXHIBITING
AT
N º 156, High Street
From SEVEN 'till TEN o'clock
JULY 1835

Admittance, 2c. each.

THE BLOODTHIRSTY BHAMPIRE

JUST ARRIVED FROM

THE HIGHLANDS;

THE GREATEST

PHŒNOMENON

Ever exhibited in this country;

Whose stay in Edinburgh will be but short.

Chapter 20

Dear Miss Bilsland,

I wish I was capable of conveniently expressing the extraordinary confusion your letter has brought me. To all your questions I cannot – sadly – offer but one single answer: Never in my life I heard of a Dr Bilsland or worked in the Highlands for a Mrs McTavish.

I am, dear Madam,
your faithful & obed. Ser.,
Mrs Luna
Madrid, 22nd August 1835

PS – I must beg of you not to waste your precious time on coming to Madrid. In my modest house you would only find a housekeeper, a young maid, a cook, a scullion boy & the French, one-handed tutor of my youngest daughter.

Acknowledgements:

This novella wouldn't have made it out to the world without the following: Mireia, with whom I discussed the very first ideas of the story and who added her talent by illustrating it. MC, who gave me not only more ideas but also the laptop on which I typed each draft. Teresa Garanhel, Anne Cleasby and all my writing companions from the Creative Writing MA at Lancaster University (2014-2015), who provided me with invaluable inspiration and helped me shape this work. Jenn Ashworth, who encouraged me with her example and support to become a professional writer and try my luck in a second language. Robert, Natasha and all the great people from the Novella Project at Holland House, who believed in this story and helped me to bring it out there. ¡Gracias!